No
Agenda

LOYD PENNINGTON

PAGE PUBLISHING, INC.
Conneaut Lake, PA

First originally published by Page Publishing 2021

ISBN 978-1-6624-2310-9 (pbk)
ISBN 978-1-6624-2311-6 (digital)

Printed in the United States of America

Introduction

IT WAS RAINING. Now, normally, that would not be a bad thing at all, especially during the middle of July in southern North Carolina when the weather was normally sweltering and as dry as toast this time of year. So, a rain shower would be more than welcome. But today, it was an unwelcome event, at least from his perspective. This was the one day he had really been looking forward to for quite a while. Today, he was up early and ready to get on the road. He was excited about the opportunity to get on his motorcycle and rendez-vous a few hours south with a lifelong friend for a week of the "road less traveled"—no agenda except to enjoy the ride.

His name was Pierce Ellis, and he was a pretty happy guy, not only today but also most every day because he had come to under-stand that to be happy was just a choice; just like which road you will take to get to a destination, you choose to be happy in the same way. That's not to say it is always easy, but then again, hardly anything that is truly worthwhile is ever easy. So, he got up every morning, and to the best of his ability, he chose to be happy and thankful.

Pierce was a good guy. He believed in doing the right thing. He really couldn't explain why he felt that way. He simply knew that at the end of the day, he would know the choices he had made, and he would sleep well. He was sure that most people felt that way and considered it a real human tragedy that the small percentage of the population who made self-centered decisions to bring economic or physical harm caused so much trouble for the vast majority who lived within the rules and pursued the common good. But he lived his life with the belief that nearly all encounters with other people along the way would be good. Again, it was a choice to see them that way and not to dwell on the negative nature of the few. There was no doubt you would have to deal with those who were selfish and bent on creating attention-getting drama that would allow them a perpetual place in the spotlight. But those were the few. He had gotten better at identifying them and steering clear of the trail of destruction they left in their wake. It was just a few after all. Most people were good at heart, and it made getting to know as many as you could quite an adventure, and Pierce had decided that the remainder of his days would be as enjoyable as he could make them. It was a very good choice.

Yet, if his life were examined and all his personal experiences noted, it would be easy to see how his perspective might not be so positive. Pierce had known a lot of difficulty in his life. He had grown up very poor without ever knowing his father, and it had taken a toll in many ways. In recent years, he had arrived at the conclusion that his father was a tortured irresponsible soul who chose to drink excessively and make self-centered decisions with no regard to their consequences to those around him. Pierce was only three years old when his father had beaten his mother in a drunken rage and left her hospitalized. When she was able to speak on the second day, she was asked by the attending physician what she "had done to deserve this." She didn't answer the absurd question. She turned away from the doctor and stared out the window at the gray skies and cried silent tears—tears that seemed to be appropriate as the raindrops slid silently down the outside of the hospital window. At that moment as the doctor noted his observations on the chart without another word, she made the decision to take her four children and get as far away from her husband as she possibly could. It was a frightening thought, but she had to protect them—a protection from physical harm—so they would never endure seeing their mother like this again.

Just one day out of the hospital and still moving gingerly as her body was slowly healing from the brutal attack, she scraped together

her meager belongings. With the help of a lady who lived next door, she sold a few things to another neighbor and bought bus tickets to escape. She could see the fear and uncertainty in the eyes and on the faces of her children. It was a gut-wrenching situation to endure, but her resolve was unwavering. Her abuser and ironically the one man she had put all her trust and faith in just a few short years ago was not even aware that she had gone till late in the evening. Even when he did realize that she and the kids had left, he made no effort to find out where she had gone. His self-absorbed way of life and lack of any real responsibility had long since robbed him, his wife, and his children of any sense of a peaceful life. It is difficult to understand why someone like him decides to wake up every day and make that decision. But the coldest decision of all was the one to never contact the woman he swore to love, honor, and cherish nor his children again. That decision had nothing to do with the kind and loving lady he had married nor with the children he fathered. It had everything to do with his own twisted sense of priorities and narcissistic personality.

Pierce's father died years later in his early fifties, alone, broke, and miserable. Pierce would receive a message to call home while serving in the US Navy. It made him anxious since that type of message almost never was good news in any form. His mom answered the phone and in a small and reluctant voice told Pierce she had some news she had to tell him. With slow and resolute words, she informed Pierce that his father had died. There was a profound kindness in her voice that spoke volumes about the person she was and the deep abiding love she had for Pierce and the rest of her children. Being told of his father's death was a bit surreal. It had little to no effect on Pierce. It was very similar to reading an obituary for someone you didn't know. It was a sad reality yet had no personal connection. There were just no feelings or emotions attached. His mother began to give him details of the arrangements that had been made, and Pierce interrupted her and said he had no intention of attending. Why would he? Throughout Pierce's life, there had never been a birthday card, a present, even a letter, or a phone call, and this individual that had chosen to live as a stranger to him and his brothers and sister had now died. So, for Pierce, he died as he had lived, with no connection to his children. It is a sad choice but his choice in the end and no one else's. But it was not lost on him how tragic it was that it meant nothing to him. Even after some quiet contemplation, Pierce made no effort to attend the service which was three states away. And truthfully, even if it were just down the street, he would not have gone either. It did occur to him that he could legitimately get some time off as bereavement leave, but he would not take that either. It just would not have felt right to do that for a man who was his father only in a biological sense. His father had never made the decision to be happy with his life and in fact couldn't do so because it would have removed one of the biggest excuses for making the bad choices that were the fabric of his existence. He chose to use the misery that was his very core to allow him to drink excessively and provide for his own destruction. It was sad, and yet in many ways, it was the lazy coward's path. The legacy of a life that could only be used as a warning and, sadly, nothing else. He was buried in a very small ceremony with few attending, and little to no tears were shed. Tears in memoriam are borne out of the loss for someone who was loved and who showered love on those important to them. Sadly, his existence never included either.

The childhood of Pierce and his brothers and sister was very difficult. There was never enough to provide for them even though his mother put forth Herculean effort. She just could not do it all on her own. Ironically, as often is the case for so many, she eventually entered a relationship with a man who was also an alcoholic. He was verbally abusive when the alcohol took over but never turned to physical violence. On several occasions, Pierce would hear his mom defend his stepfather by pointing out that "at least, he didn't hit her." How bizarre to excuse behavior that is not only self-destructive but also detrimental to all that surround them as not being as bad as it could have been. His twin vices of drinking and smoking were as much a part of him as his hair color, small stature, or any other physical attribute. In many ways, they defined him. There was always money to provide for these "needs" regardless of other obligations that others might see as logically more pressing.

When Pierce was just eleven years old, his shoes had literally torn apart during recess at school. The sole of the shoe was separated from the upper part to the point that only about ten percent of the area held the shoot together. When he took a step, it slapped loudly on the bottom of his foot and showed the large hole in his sock. He had embarrassingly returned to the classroom alone and used the stapler in an attempt to repair his shoe with hopes it would get him home. It did. That night after a few beers, his disgusted stepfather had remarked to him that his shoe would not have fallen apart if he hadn't been out there "kicking them balls and running around." Even at eleven years old, he understood that this was absurd but still felt very guilty and found a quiet place to cry. It stands as a very stark reminder that words are indeed powerful. Some, both good and bad, will echo through the canyons of time. Some will encourage and energize an individual throughout their life's journey, while others, like these spoken to an eleven-year-old boy, whose only offense was to act like an eleven-year-old boy, would prove to be so powerful that they would never be forgotten.

Pierce would try to wear a dilapidated old pair of shoes from his older brother, but they were three sizes too large and ridiculous. He would have to stay out of school the remainder of the week since there would be no money until after payday on Friday. It was difficult, and it was not lost on the young man that every night a twelve-pack of beer and cigarettes came into the house. The cost for a pair of the cheap shoes he wore would not even have totaled just one night's beer and cigarette expense. It was hard for an eleven-year-old to understand that choice. But after a few unscheduled days of being home alone, Saturday came, and another cheap pair of shoes were purchased. It would cross his mind from time to time to try to take better care of those shoes even though it seemed to be against the natural order of things for a young energetic boy. The experience had a profound effect and served as a very valuable lesson as he grew older, and Pierce would choose never to drink or smoke. It was also that incident that had caused him to make the silent promise to himself that if he ever had children, he would always choose his words carefully and do all he could to provide for them.

Difficult Days

PIERCE HAD ALSO survived the divorce of a marriage of fifteen years. Those days of dealing with the end of the relationship and all the turmoil that surrounded it was a time in his life that often challenged his very desire to go on. And even though he spent so many days stumbling through a numbing fog that seemed to somehow provide a shield against the enormity of it all, he pressed on. He found comfort in the fact that although the pain seemed unbearable at times, without it, he would never have had the kids who were the anchor that had held him steady during those turbulent days and especially the long lonely nights.

Two of these precious souls were not his biological children, but he loved them just the same, and he had spent as much time with them as work and life would allow and loved the role of dad. It was so important that he do it well. He understood fully that he was not their father but felt he could serve their daily needs as their dad. He needed to prove to himself that the role was worthy, and he was capable regardless of the actions of his own father and never having had a role model in that regard. He had chosen to love these two precious people and did so without holding anything back while knowing full well that there would be times when his heart would be broken. When the challenges of life stepped in as they became strong independent people, if he had done the job right, he would know the difficulty would ultimately serve them well. It was part of the journey, and he was willing to endure the tough days. Pierce never regretted the decision to give his heart to them. The reward was worth the battle. And maybe, the greater truth was that he did so due to his own core belief that it was the right thing to do and the highest calling of any man.

After being married to his wife for a few years, Pierce became more and more aware of a deep and moving desire to have a biological child of his own. This continued for a couple of years, the desire grew, and one day, he discussed it with his wife. She surprised him when she was also excited about the prospect. With her in agreement, Pierce spent the days after in deep contemplation, and one day soon thereafter, alone in the woods, he fell to his knees and made a promise to God that if he would give him his own child, he would be the very best father he could be. Some would say it was just a fifty-fifty chance, but throughout the pregnancy, though he told no one about his strong feeling, Pierce was absolutely sure he would have a son.

On the day his son was born and he held him for the first time as he breathed his first breath, he knew that without hesitation, he would give his own life for this new life that was truly an answer to his prayer. He would be a good father to this child and the two children who already were living in the house they called home. He would make that choice every day. It brought him tremendous satisfaction even during the trials and tribulations of life.

In those early days of caring for this precious child, he often reflected on the events, decisions, his own, and those individuals in his past that had brought him to those days. One of those would have profoundly affected all of them. It could have taken them down a very different path.

Pierce had been offered a job when the two oldest kids were almost teenagers. The youngest, his son, was not yet born. The job offer was in a location nearly a thousand miles away. The offer and the way it all came about were both thrilling and a bit overwhelming. He had been highly recommended by an executive of a firm that he worked closely with as one of his vendors at his current job. They worked well together in a professional capacity, but Pierce was not aware that he thought so highly of him. It was both humbling and very flattering. One day, the CEO of that company had surprised him by calling him personally. After a very pleasant conversation, he had asked Pierce to come to their facility to interview. It was indeed gratifying, and it seemed prudent to go and see what the job entailed. Nothing ventured, nothing gained. This small-town boy from such humble beginnings that he often went to bed hungry and even missed school because he had no shoes was being courted in such a grand way. Just two days later, they had sent a private jet to the local airport and flown him to the corporate office. He was a little shocked when the sleek jet came down the runway, and he realized it was for him. He was told they had their own "plane," but the small jet was impressive enough to raise the eyebrows of those at the small regional airport that morning. And for Pierce, to be able to climb aboard and be the only passenger was a thrilling experience indeed. It was hard for him to wrap his head around it all, but he tried very hard to savor every moment.

The flight took only an hour. The company's regional manager met him at the airport to take him to the location. His name was Bill, and he was a very pleasant but a no-nonsense kind of guy. He provided some more insight into the company, its goals, and how he came to be a part of the team. In the twenty-five minutes it took to arrive at the facility, Pierce was feeling pretty comfortable with his understanding of the position and the company he was interviewing with today. As they pulled through the gate of the expansive property in the rural setting, it was easy to see that the expectations for excellence had been established. The grounds were immaculate and well maintained. He and Bill were met in the lobby by several others, and there was a quick tour of the facility that they would be his new home if things worked out.

After the tour concluded, Pierce joined Bill, the CEO Gary, and a couple of others in the conference room for a very nice lunch and informal conversation. From his perspective, they said all the right things, and he hoped they were feeling that as well regarding him. They certainly appeared to be impressed by his visit. After the plates had been removed and more of the formal process of the interview had taken place, Gary thanked the others and let them go on their way. Pleasantries were exchanged, and everyone but Gary and Pierce left the conference room. After a few more questions, an offer was made with salary and benefits being more than he had hoped. There were also the added incentive and lots of perks as well. Pierce later remembered thinking at that point that the harsher winters would be more acceptable for a southern boy with all that was being offered. It was overwhelming and a bit surreal as he tried to process it all without looking like a wide-eyed kid on Christmas morning. The poor kid who had scratched his way to this day was finally going to be somebody. It felt good. He could not believe his good fortune and knew he could handle the job responsibilities. He had somehow managed to maintain his outward confidence even as the endless negative "what-ifs" were swirling in his mind. But he steadied himself, looked this very astute and professional gentleman in the eye, and gave him a firm handshake as he stood to thank him graciously for the consideration and their hospitality. They stood and walked to the door. Smiles and even a pat on the back from the CEO told him he had indeed made the impression on them he had sought.

On the way back to the airport in the back of the cab that had arrived for him, he couldn't help but smile. He sat at the airport waiting to depart, and all that had just happened ran on a continuous loop in his mind. The details of what needed to happen next were starting to take shape as the time came to board and head back home. But not long after the wheels were up, he thought of the two kids, the two, that even though they shared no genetic bond, he considered his kids. They had been through so much in their young lives, and the last couple of years of stability and continuity had had a positive effect on them both. The realization that Pierce couldn't bear the thought of telling them they were going to be uprooted again washed over him bringing him back from the whirlwind fantasy. It would mean a different house, a different city, a different school, and trying to make new friends all over again. How would that ultimately affect them?

And of course, what about his family? They all lived within twenty miles of each other, and after the passing of his stepfather a couple of years back, they got together almost every Sunday afternoon for lunch and to stay connected. It was the anchor that held him moored to the comfort and peace of a simple life. He knew before the jet touched down again that he wouldn't take the job. There was a resolute certainty even as he felt somewhat torn about what might have been. And it was so very flattering. Pierce was thankful for that chance to be recognized for the work ethic that was at the core of all his days.

And so now a few years later, as he sat reflecting about the birth of his son and having been able to spend that time with his family, especially his sister, he felt comfortable that it was the right decision. It was a good choice that he would look back on and ponder from time to time but with no real regrets.

Sissie

PIERCE HAD ENDURED the loss of his younger sister just a few short months ago. It had been very sudden, for one day she was there, and it seemed she always would be, and the next day, she was gone forever. She was the anchor of the family. She was the planner, the caretaker, and the source of endless projects—projects that very seldom were for her own benefit except for the joy she got to witness on the faces of those around her. It had been years since she had seen a whole movie, and she almost never watched TV. Her energy level was unmatched, and it occurred to Pierce as he worked on the obituary that would be placed in the paper that just maybe she had accomplished so many selfless worthwhile endeavors in her short life and did so much real good and that it was all that God had required of her.

Pierce truly missed his sister every day. It seemed unfair that it took losing her to allow him to understand just how precious she was to him.

They called her Sissie, and Pierce was not ashamed in any way of the many tears he had shed since that day that he had lost her. She was worth every tear and so much more. How was it possible that he couldn't pick up the phone and call her?

So, Pierce was more determined than ever to find ways to be very *intentional* about enjoying his life, taking nothing for granted, and showing those around him that he held dear, that he loved them.

It had become a word that he thought about every day, *intentional*. It was the resolute idea that you could choose to deal with the aspects of your life head-on. To Pierce, it was very much like white-water rafting. The flow of life would be turbulent at times, but little corrections and choices to deal with the current along the way would make all the difference as the journey unfolded. It was the difference between an exciting enjoyable ride and a terror-filled trek that left you wondering how you could possibly get through it all—little choices, little corrections, and being very *intentional* about enjoying the gift of each passing day.

Although Pierce was divorced and kiddingly stated many times that he would never be a "victim" of marriage again, he had married the sweetest girl he had ever known just three weeks before. It was a small but appropriate ceremony.

Lynn

Lynn was a lovely, passionate, and caring lady with a dazzling smile. She was funny, thoughtful, and kind, and whenever Pierce was with her, he knew they would enjoy just being together. She was a natural beauty with a stunning face and gorgeous figure. She could light up a room and had stolen his heart although he had guarded it so closely. It was very evident that even the men who tried to make it appear otherwise clearly took notice when she was around.

Lynn and Pierce had known each other through mutual friends and community events. He always enjoyed their conversations and her keen intellect laced with a refreshing sense of humor. Even though it would sometimes be months between their encounters, there was always a sense of warm comfort in her presence. Later, when both found themselves single, they had talked on the phone, but it seemed very unlikely they would ever go past that. As time went on, he would realize that he cared so much for her as a person that he was afraid that his strong belief that he would never be able to truly commit to anyone again would only end up hurting her. He couldn't stand that thought. So, they would go for periods of time without talking to each other. On numerous occasions, Pierce had hoped she would find someone else who would be able to be the companion he felt he couldn't be but that her heart deserved. Luckily for Pierce, that never happened, and they started seeing each other seriously last year. They were doing very well, and he didn't allow himself to consider the "what-ifs" at all. It was good. He knew how blessed he was to have her in his life.

And yet as time passed, there was not a single day that he didn't relive that early Sunday morning when the call came. It was his brother on the other end, and without explanation, his brother blurted out, "You need to come to the hospital." Pierce's first thought was that his grandmother must be sick again. She was nearly ninety-three and had been in and out of the hospital for the last few months. But then, he heard the words that would stun him and ring in his head every day thereafter. His brother said, "They brought Sissie here last night, and well, you need to get on up here." There was something in his voice that was as unfamiliar as if it were someone he didn't know at all. He knew it wasn't good. He hung up the phone and began to rush around. Pierce heard himself say out loud, "Sissie?" Why would they bring Sissie there? Without a doubt, she was certainly fine. She had to be fine. He dressed as quickly as possible, and he drove to the hospital.

A thousand possibilities ran through his mind on the way, and not one involved her being gone. He caught himself driving far too fast several times and forced himself to slow down as his thoughts came out in fragments that made no sense. He seemed to sense what had happened.

When he arrived at the hospital, he was asking the lady at the desk where he could find her when a very mild-mannered man who had overheard him saying the name of the person he was trying to locate put his hand gently on his shoulder and said, "I am so sorry for your loss."

Pierce spun around as if the man had stabbed him and looked at him wide-eyed and said, "Loss? What do you mean loss?" but the nurse had her hand on his back and was already moving him down the hall to the room where the rest of the family had been gathered. The next few hours were almost unbearable as the reality of the fact that his sister was gone scratched its way into his world. The world in which he had gotten up every day and tried so hard to be happy was now in a state of bizarre chaos. He knew that there would always be a part of him that would struggle to comprehend the world without his sister.

Lynn had a lot of the same giving and caring attributes of his sister. He hated that she never had the chance to know her but knew without a doubt that she would have loved her. He knew he cared for Lynn very deeply, but for the first time, he allowed himself to feel the pain that he would have to live through if she weren't there. Suddenly, it was crystal clear that his life would not be complete without his very best friend, and so, he asked her to marry him. The realization of the incredible person that he had found in Lynn combined with the clarity of the brevity of life allowed him to experience a deep abiding love that naturally made him want this natural bond. And the gift of love that he had chosen to ignore out of fear was abundantly clear. Releasing that fear had brought him a sincere incomparable joy.

They had chosen to have a simple private ceremony, and their life together was very good. It seemed odd to be leaving for a week so soon after being married, but Lynn knew he had planned the trip almost a year ago, and although she gave him that cute pout several times, she seemed to be alright and even very supportive with his taking the trip.

So, Pierce checked out his gear strapped to his bike, making sure that it was all secure and that he hadn't forgotten anything. It looked like everything would be fine.

Pierce loved his motorcycle. It was a 2014 Indian Chief Vintage. An American-made motorcycle with a 111-cubic-inch engine and very comfortably accessorized to make a cruise like this very enjoyable. It was a head-turning color called Indian red that he had never seen on another bike before he found the Indian. He had spent months researching the resurrection of the classic badge with so much history. Indian had built the bike which was the very first American motorcycle, and Pierce loved the story, the quality, and the attention to the heritage of the name. It had aftermarket exhaust pipes that most women would consider too loud and most bike enthusiasts would consider more beautiful than even the most expertly crafted symphony. He loved the feeling of freedom that the bike gave him.

It had been a welcome form of therapy during those days when life didn't make sense and just a whole lot of fun on so many others. It would be good to be spending the next few days on her.

He so wanted to get going. The ride had been planned almost a year ago, and there had been five of his closest friends who would be riding together. But as the time got closer, life's other priorities had intervened for all but Pierce and Sam. Since Sam lived outside Orlando, they had agreed to meet in Savannah, Georgia, which was a good halfway point for both.

Sam

SAM WAS MORE important to Pierce than he would ever know. They had been friends since elementary school. There were so many great times spent together as they were growing up and trying to find their place in the world and so many adventures they had shared, many of which even now they couldn't tell their kids about. But through it all, there was an unspoken bond that was as real as the chrome and steel they would ride. It was the best part of the trip. A couple of years back, when Pierce was single and living alone, Sam had come over and sat on the front porch with him for hours the night before he was facing surgery. It was a necessary surgery that would reveal whether the tumors that were being removed meant a cancer diagnosis. Both tumors would turn out to be benign, but Pierce would never be able to express his gratitude for Sam being there during those hours of trepidation the night before. Sam claimed he was only there for the sweet tea, but Pierce knew better, although Pierce had paid close attention to his mother and did indeed make some good southern iced tea. And though it was a surprise at the time, it shouldn't have been that Sam put everything on hold to fly in to be at Sissie's funeral. But that was Sam, he was there without hesitation. He was real. It was Pierce's greatest hope that his children would make friends who would be as important to them as the friends Pierce had found in his own life. And certainly, there was none more important than Sam.

Time to Go

THE RAIN HAD diminished to a steady drizzle so Pierce decided he had waited as long as he could. The radar on his laptop revealed the rain stretching north but ending just south of where he was. Since the entire ride today was heading south, he would only be wet for a little while. His sense of urgency had taken over, and it was time to go.

Lynn was not happy about his leaving while it was still raining but knew enough not to try to change his mind when the man she married was in his "kid mode." The excitement in his eyes told her he was on his way. She asked if he had his cell phone. Was it set to vibrate? Did he check his tire pressure? Did he have his earbuds and music all set? He gave her his best "yes, dear" look, and she kissed him—not a quick kiss but a kiss that says *I really do love you*, and the way he held her and looked deeply into her eyes was evidence that even though he was clearly excited to go, he really would miss her. The kiss gave her tingles, and it felt good. Once again, she found herself awash in gratitude for the unique bond that they shared.

She watched him start the bike, which she thought was too loud, and ride down the driveway and turn onto the road. She would stand on the porch and listen to the sound until she couldn't hear it anymore. He would be careful, she knew that, but she couldn't say she wouldn't worry about him. Even Pierce was quick to admit that motorcycles were inherently dangerous, but he was just as quick to point out that many people slipped and died in the bathtub every year. "If I'm going to go, I will be much happier doing so on the bike rather than with a loofah stuck up my butt!" It made her smile. She loved the fact that he made her laugh. There was no activity involving motors and wheels which was perfectly safe, but still, she hoped he would be careful of all the others on the road. The "knuckleheads" as he liked to call them. But even through her twinge of knowing she would miss him and genuine concern, she hoped he had a great time. He worked hard and deserved this time to get away from his normal hectic routine.

Lynn went inside and poured her second cup of coffee and settled on the couch to look at her social media sites. She would take a little time for herself and then get some laundry going. She would probably miss church this morning, but she would be productive and get some housework done and see if she could catch up with her sister-in-law later so they could have lunch together. It was only 7:00 a.m. There was plenty of time to enjoy the coffee and find out what was going on in the world before getting busy with the chores.

On the Road

Pierce was finally on the road. The rain was very light and not so bad except for the fact that the three hours he had spent cleaning every inch of the bike the day before were now wasted. But of course, it wasn't supposed to rain. The forecast was for cloudy skies but no rain at all—another example of why he wasn't really sure why he bothered watching the weather. They were so often wrong. Too many times, he had thought that the state of the American economic engine would be pretty dismal if everyone could be wrong as often as the so-called meteorologists were. Yet, they were still allowed to speak with authority the next day as if they were previously right. But were they taken off the air, he would miss the weather lady on channel 18; she was far too attractive not to forgive, so he guessed you take the good with the bad? He smiled to himself, and just as that thought had rolled through his mind, he realized that though he was only a few miles down the road, it was no longer raining.

Pierce was headed South on Highway 521 with plans to pick up Highway 9 East and then 601 South which he had noted on the map just yesterday, going most of the way to Savannah. He was excited to find a route that didn't include the interstate. Interstates are simply no fun on a motorcycle. And this trip was about having fun and enjoying the ride itself since there was no specific destination after meeting Sam this afternoon. ZZ Top came on his MP3 player, and he smiled and rolled the throttle a little more just to feel the power. This was going to be a good day and a good week.

Pierce had been riding about thirty minutes when he came to the point where Highway 9 intersects with 601 South. He was aware that it was already getting warm, and the light jacket that he needed in the rain now was getting uncomfortable, but he didn't want to stop. He would put some miles behind him before he would take a break and put it in the saddlebag. It was then he remembered he had forgotten to take the two large rolls of duct tape out that he had picked up the day before. He had needed it, and since he passed the hardware store on the way to gas up, he picked them up. It was a simple fact of life: you never know when you might need duct tape. He had often told his friends that if duct tape had been invented in time, the Titanic would never have sunk, and the Wright brothers would have been flying a lot sooner.

This was a great road choice, and he couldn't help but smile. He glanced down at the clock and noted it was not even 8 a.m., and that would explain why there was no traffic whatsoever on the road on this bright Sunday morning in the middle of July. It would be mid-nineties by the afternoon, but with a little luck, he would be in Savannah before the worst of the heat set in.

As he rounded a curve in the road, he grabbed the brakes and quickly downshifted. There was a car that was half in and half out of the road. It appeared to have just stopped there, and as he slowly went around it, he noticed a young lady in the driver's seat. Although he was anxious to put some miles behind him, he certainly couldn't leave her there. He saw the edge of the road looked firm enough, so he stopped and parked the bike and removed his helmet. Pierce walked back to the car. He smiled as he approached and said, "Can I help you?" The young lady, who appeared to be a teenager and likely a new driver, looked very nervous and through a window lowered only about three inches said, "No, I called my Dad, and he is on his way. I think I ran out of gas." He realized she was just being cautious so Pierce said, "How about if I just push you out of the road so it will be a little safer until he gets here?" She was shifting nervously so Pierce gave her his best smile and said, "You can stay in the car and just steer so we get you out of the road?" So, she nodded and said, "Okay." Pierce made his way to the back of the car and asked her to put the car in neutral and take her foot off the brake. But try as he would, the car wouldn't budge. He couldn't understand it; the road was flat, and the side of the road was even a little lower. This was challenging his ego. At six feet tall and 215 pounds, he should be able to move this car a few feet to safety without a lot of effort. He stopped trying to push and approached the window of the car, and as he started to ask her if the car was in *neutral*, he saw it was in *drive*. He explained it needed to be in the "N" position, which was neutral. She shifted the car, and it moved a little immediately. "Make sure you don't have your foot on the brake," he said in his most patient tone. Pierce got behind the car once again and easily moved it the few feet to get it off the road. The young lady smiled and said, "Thanks," but Pierce could see she was still unsure of his intentions so he told her he would go wait by his motorcycle until her dad arrived. He liked that she was being very cautious and smiled as he walked back to his bike. He did not look for her approval nor wait for her to say it was OKAY for him to wait. It was simply the right thing to do.

Pierce had his bike on the grassy shoulder of the road and was standing in the tall grass that was up to his knees. He took the opportunity to remove his jacket and put it in his saddlebag. He had only been there for a few minutes when an older white pickup truck pulled up behind the car. He saw the look of relief on the young lady's face and knew immediately it was her father. He nodded politely to both, put his helmet back on, and got back on his bike to continue. He hadn't noticed that hidden in the tall grass, there was a fire ant mound, and he had been standing on the edge of it. Even now, there were quite a few fire ants covering the whole lower half of his right boot. He started the bike and got back on the road heading south.

Pierce had only been riding for a few miles when the fire ants made their way to the top of his boot, and irritated by the heat from the engine, they began to scurry down inside his boot. He felt the sharp fiery pain of the first bite and then another. By the third bite, he was in considerable pain. More and more of the little devils bit his lower leg and ankle, and the reason they were called fire ants was abundantly clear. He recognized a familiar brown park sign ahead on his right, 40 Acre Rock. It was a small, seldom used park that had a gravel parking area a couple of hundred yards up the left side of this road. He knew he had to stop to get some relief from the pain that was now excruciating. He needed to find out the cause and try to get some relief. He didn't know that he had now been bitten dozens of times. But he understood that he needed to find some relief from the burning pain. He made the sharp right turn back up the road and, as he remembered, found the parking area he had visited a few times before.

The pain was torrid now, and he had a good idea as to the source. The south had been invaded several years back by the tiny terrors, and he knew the pain from unfortunate previous experiences. He pulled into the empty parking area and stopped as quickly as possible. He leaped off the bike and grabbed his boot and pulled it off. Just as he suspected, there were tiny fire ants there and numerous bite marks on his ankle and leg. They had already turned into nasty little raised blisters. He grabbed a water bottle from his saddlebag and dumped the water down his leg and foot. It helped a little, so he grabbed the other two and did the same with them. He would pick up more somewhere down the road. He looked down at his watch. It was already almost 8:30, and he was getting nowhere fast. He was really going to need to be rolling to get back on his schedule. He made sure there were no more ants in the boot, on his sock, or any-where else on him.

Pierce was both blessed and cursed with an innate, strong sense of urgency that was taking him over now. He absolutely hated being late for anything. Most of his friends did not understand this urgent way to see things. They would remind him to relax and ask why he was so concerned about being a little late. To explain the logic of his sense of urgency, he had often used this question. If someone said you had won $100,000 and all you had to do was be in a specific place at a specific time to pick it up, but being late would cause you to forfeit the prize, what time would you be there? Of course, you would leave early and do whatever was necessary to be there on time. Why? Because it was important for you to be on time. So, when you show up late, you are simply saying it isn't important enough to be there on time. It was a matter of disrespect. He had gotten better as he aged not to hold others to the same strict standard that he held himself, but he couldn't change his need to do precisely what he had said he would. Again, it was both a blessing and a curse. He had to get everything back together and find a way to make up some time. Now, his overpowering thought was that he had to put this bike in the wind and push that threshold of a speeding ticket to get back on track! He smiled as the idea of he, the bike, and ZZ Top burning up the road came over him.

Jacob Chandler

Jacob wanted to be a police officer for as long as he could remember. He was one of those kids who would later go to his ten-year reunion, and many would not remember. He wasn't an athlete and not a scholar either. He didn't join any clubs and was basically just another face in the hall at Camden High School. He had chosen to walk in the shadows rather than to find a place to shine. He was certainly not a bad kid in any way; he just never did anything that was very memorable. He didn't stand out from the crowd. That may well be why he wanted to be a police officer. After graduating from high school, Jacob worked on his parent's farm. It was hard work, but he knew it well and the idea of helping the family appealed to him. But as time went on, his desire to pursue his dream of being in law enforcement burned in him till one day, he sat down with his folks and told them what he wanted to do with his life. They were very supportive, and he went about planning to attend the necessary school and training. It was a very proud day for him and his family when Jacob was sworn in as an officer for the police force of Camden South Carolina. He hoped he could put in a couple of years and then apply to be a highway patrol officer which was his ultimate goal.

Jacob Chandler was an only child born to third-generation farming parents. It was a simple, quiet life that he was thankful for, but Jacob wanted to stand out, to be looked up to for something. Being a police officer provided that experience, and even though he was just two months into the job, he knew it was a good choice for him.

Being the new guy on a small force was a little tough at times. He had to endure a lot of jokes about "the rookie" and even was forced to tolerate being the butt of a few practical jokes, but he figured it came with the territory and never let it get to him. He drew the shifts no one else wanted, and such was the case with this shift that had been very quiet and only had a couple more hours left. It was from midnight Saturday until noon on Sunday. It had been mostly quiet, and now, at just after 9:00 a.m., he had started to see a few more cars making their way around town and a few cars he didn't recognize passing through. *Probably tourists on their way to the beach*, he thought. They saw lots of those this time of year. He had been sitting in the parking lot at Emily's Diner for a while and had just thought about moving on. The chief didn't like for them to sit in one spot too long: "You need to be seen patrolling, boys, not parking." He said it a lot. So, Jacob started the car.

Jacob watched as a guy on a red motorcycle with beautiful leather seats and saddlebags passed by. He nodded to the guy as he did to everyone that he made eye contact with, but the guy didn't seem to notice. The motorcycle had bags strapped onto it and was apparently just another tourist passing through. He pulled onto the road and headed south of town toward I-20 where he would turn around and make the loop through that part of town.

As he rode a short distance behind the motorcycle, he noticed the sound as the rider changed gears. It sounded good, and he made a mental note to have one of those, one day. It just seemed like fun. It might be fun too for his friends to be shocked once again as the "bad boy" came out in him. He smiled at the thought.

Jacob was approaching a stoplight that was already yellow, and both he and the bike were forced to stop.

Brian Trainor was the officer coming on duty, and suddenly, the car radio came to life. "Hey, Jake, where are you?" It startled Jacob a little, and he fumbled with the mic grabbing it quickly. "Headed south, just making the loop; you're at work early. Didn't expect to hear from you until 11:59." "Okay, rookie," Brian said, "just be sure to gas up the patrol car before you come in. I have to use it today. I am headed to the early service with the little lady and was just swinging by to get my uniform so I can change at home before going on patrol." Jacob replied, "Roger that. See you shortly," and hung up the mic.

The light turned green, and the bike pulled away with Jacob a short distance behind. It gave Jacob a certain sense of power to ride behind someone in the patrol car. Almost without fail, they would be going exactly the speed limit or maybe a mile or two below it. Such was the case with the motorcycle in front of him. He was traveling at exactly thirty-five mph.

"Hey, rookie," came the sound from the radio again. "Don't forget to leave me a nice snack in the car, and none of those generic cookies either; I am thinking maybe a nice piece of red velvet cake from Emily's Diner."

Jacob replied, "10-4." It was just another part of the process—hazing in its mildest form—and Jacob really didn't mind. But the smile quickly vanished when he noticed the motorcycle in front of him wobbling and almost crossing the center line as the rider seemed to be reaching for something in his pocket. And then, the bike suddenly accelerated. Within a few seconds, it was far out ahead of Jacob's patrol car and already almost to the I-20 ramp.

Jacob felt the adrenaline rush as he realized that the quiet morning had suddenly ended, and he was about to be in his first high-speed chase. He turned on the lights and siren and jumped on the gas to try to catch up. He was closing the gap a little and knew he needed to call in the pursuit. He glanced down at the speedometer and realized he was going a little over a hundred miles per hour. He was shaking as he gripped the steering wheel tightly. Just as he was grabbing the mic, the bike swerved wildly as it appeared to lose control making a last-second decision to stay on 601 rather than take the I-20 ramp onto the interstate. He watched in horror as the motorcycle veered off the road. The bike and the rider seemed to be at odds with each other as the man's limbs moved in all directions. Then, without warning, there was a sudden impact on the guardrail and then on the concrete support of the overpass. The motorcycle literally flew apart, and there were pieces of it scattering in all directions. For a few moments, time was frozen, and it seemed to Jacob that he was watching this take place in front of him as if it were some movie, and yet, this was all too real. Jacob slowed the car as quickly as he could and approached the scene in disbelief as it became evident that the rider had been literally torn apart as well. Just as Jacob got to the scene and leaped from his car, he saw the front part of the bike go up in flames. He ran toward the burning hunk of metal nearly tripping over the helmet still spinning slowly on the pavement and realized that the top part of the rider's torso was underneath the flames and the lower half was one hundred feet away. Without warning, he vomited violently.

Ed Wallace

Ed Wallace had been with the South Carolina Highway Patrol for almost twenty-two years, and he had never seen anything like this.

He had been at the top of the on-ramp where 601 South meets I-20 East. He had stopped a young girl in a black Honda Civic for swerving erratically. He was leaning into the car and giving her a stern warning about how dangerous it was to text while driving. Once he ruled out being under the influence, he felt sure it was the cause of her driving so badly. It didn't appear that she had been drinking, and texting was all too common these days. He had just asked her if she was weaving due to texting when he heard the crash. Seconds later, he saw the smoke rising from underneath the overpass and without another word to the young girl; he turned and ran to his cruiser. With the lights already on, he turned on the siren and executed a U-turn heading the wrong way down the ramp.

It was difficult at first to take in what his eyes were trying to relay to him. There was a local squad car already there, and an officer standing nearby with his hands on his knees looking down at the ground. And then, he was shocked by the realization of what had just occurred.

Jacob looked up and saw Officer Wallace getting out of his car. He tried to steady himself and stood upright. He heard himself say, "I'll call an ambulance." But Officer Wallace just looked at him and said, "No, son. We need to close the road from both sides and get the coroner on the way; an ambulance won't be of any help now." Officer Wallace was hurrying toward the fire with a small fire extinguisher from his cruiser. He was trying to be careful not to step on the pieces of the wreckage strewn in all directions. He knew the immediate need was to attend to the fire if he could and then to take care of securing the scene. It was an incredible sight that he couldn't really take in. He simply had to act. The smell of the gasoline and flesh burning was enough to stop you in your tracks all by itself.

As he approached the blazing hunk tucked closely to the concrete support, he was able to maneuver around the side of it and managed to knock down the flames. It was a gut-wrenching sight to see the top half of what was the rider just moments before, now totally engulfed in flames. In the distance, he heard the wailing siren of an approaching fire truck.

After requesting backup and the Volunteer Fire Department, Jacob had grabbed the large roll of yellow police line caution tape from the patrol car and was trying to figure out how best to use it to secure the area of the wreck. For just a motorcycle, it covered a large area. He looked to his left at the edge of the road and stared in disbelief as he took in the sight of the pair of Wrangler jeans with the black boots at the bottom. One boot was turned the opposite of the other, twisted in an unnatural position so that it looked like one-half of a Halloween decoration, except for the fact that it was one-half of the rider he had been calmly following just minutes before. His mind reeled wildly, *What had happened here?* He hadn't even turned on his lights or siren when the motorcyclist had sped away. It didn't make any sense, and he felt the bile rising in his throat again and felt a little dizzy. He leaned back against the car to allow the feeling to pass.

Soon, there was a multitude of cars and people everywhere. The fire truck had arrived and taken care of what was left of the fire that had spread to the dry grass along the roadway. The road had been closed, and volunteer firemen were directing traffic away from the scene. Sheets had been draped over the two areas where the majority of what was left of the body were. They were waiting on the coroner to arrive to process the scene and "pick up the pieces," so to speak. To say it would be a grisly task was a gross understatement. Officer

Wallace walked over to Jacob and put his arm around his shoulder. "Son, don't you feel bad about this at all? You and I will have to put together a report of what happened here, but I promise nothing in it will be embarrassing to you. I have served twenty-two years next week, and I was close to losing my breakfast on this one. Why was he running?" Jacob told Officer Wallace every detail of how it had happened from the very first minute he saw the bright-red motorcycle. Why the motorcycle had suddenly accelerated and crashed was a mystery that they may never know since the only person who could tell them was gone forever. Why he made that choice would haunt Jacob every day for the rest of his life. It was a story he would tell again and again not only this day but also in the weeks ahead and for many years to come.

Verification

THE CORONER ARRIVED and with the help of several officers had begun the task of processing the scene. He noted that this was a single-vehicle accident with one victim, although the upper half of the body had been burned severely and the head crushed on impact from contact with the concrete support. He had retrieved the wallet from the rear pants pocket of the jeans and found multiple items there identifying the victim as one Pierce Richard Ellis. The cell phone found in the right front pocket was amazingly still functional and displayed one text message delivered just a short time ago which, according to the information given to him, was approximately at the time of the crash. It was still unread. He opened it up and read the message. It said just three words, "I love you!" and was from Lynn. He would have to contact local authorities in North Carolina and have them give this lady the bad news. As bad as this part of the job was, he was glad he didn't have to do that.

Caldwell and Newell

THE CALL CAME in, and all the information was relayed about a horrific motorcycle crash that had taken the life of a local man. Officers Caldwell and Newell would have to be the ones to go and speak to the wife of the deceased. They had just returned from lunch and hoped to spend the rest of their shift quietly finishing paperwork and preparing for the next day. But they both had been at this long enough to know that you never know the direction your day will take. But this was one of those tasks that you couldn't prepare for and just had to get through.

They drove the hour it took to get to the address given. Although there was a truck in the driveway, there didn't appear to be anyone home. Just as they were returning from knocking on the door without a response, a car pulled into the driveway.

Lynn had met her sister-in-law for lunch and was returning home. She wondered how far Pierce had gotten and was thinking about how she would spend the rest of her day. She felt herself smiling as she contemplated taking the hammock Pierce had put up a few days before, for a little "test ride." It was Sunday afternoon after all, and a short nap seemed appropriate.

As Lynn approached the house, she saw a county police car parked out front and felt a sense of fear rise up in her. She wondered if the house had been broken into and the alarm had gone off. But wait, she didn't set the alarm before she left. She pulled into the driveway and saw the two officers standing there. The sullen look on their faces caused everything to start to move in slow motion, and she would remember that look for the rest of her life.

Officer Caldwell felt that sick feeling in his gut as he went to open the door of the car for the lady inside who looked very scared and concerned. "Hi there. Are you Mrs. Ellis?" he asked. Lynn could only nod her head. "Is there something wrong?" she asked. Officer Newell looked at her and said, "Ma'am, if we could just go inside for a few minutes, we need to ask you a couple of questions, and it's awfully hot out here. Would that be okay?" He tried to give her his most reassuring smile, but the news he was there to deliver simply wouldn't allow that to happen. Lynn replied, "Sure, but what is this about? Is everything alright?" Officer Newell replied, "Let's just go inside, and we can be more comfortable to talk there. It's a real scorcher out here, isn't it?" So, Lynn hesitantly walked over to the door and unlocked it. The two officers followed her in.

Lynn felt a rising tide of panic as she sat down and couldn't contain herself any longer. She heard herself say, "Why are you here, and what is going on? Please tell me now!" It was much louder than she had intended, but she didn't care. She was locked in on the two officers, not sure who would speak first.

Officer Caldwell said, "Let's just have a seat." Reluctantly, Lynn sat in one of the chairs at the kitchen table and gestured for them to sit as well. Officer Caldwell began by asking, "Mrs. Ellis, is your husband Pierce Ellis?" Lynn responded, "Yes." She felt as if her body was numb. "When was the last time you spoke to your husband?" Lynn felt a tear running down her cheek as the inevitable news seemed to get closer. She replied, "It was this morning when he was leaving to go on a trip on his motorcycle. Is he okay?" She knew the answer before she asked it but simply wanted to believe that there was some chance that Pierce was alright.

"Can you describe his motorcycle, ma'am?"

"Describe his motorcycle?" Lynn screamed, "Tell me right now if my husband is OKAY!" Officer Caldwell looked her in the eyes and, with a catch in his voice, said, "I am so sorry to inform you that your husband was killed in an accident earlier today." The next few minutes are a mystery to her now. She has no recollection of the conversation at all. She knows she was crying, and she asked what had happened, but it was as if it was all happening to someone else. How could this be? They were just getting their life started.

Officers Caldwell and Newell worked through the questions they needed answers for to file the paperwork. What was he wearing? What time did he leave? Which direction was he going? What was his intended destination? What were the make and model of the motorcycle and the tag that was simple since it was a personalized plate? Everything was checked out. It was just another sad story. Officer Caldwell said, "We will stay with you until someone gets here. Who can we call for you?" Just as he was in midsentence, her phone rang. It was her sister-in-law. She answered it, and without saying hello, she blurted out, "Pierce is gone," and she began to wail as the reality came down on her. Officer Caldwell gently took the phone from her hand and began to speak to the lady on the other end of the call. He told her only the most necessary detail and asked if she could come and be with Lynn. She replied, "Of course, I can be there in fifteen minutes."

"Good," Officer Caldwell replied. "We will wait until you get here before we leave."

Lynn was crying uncontrollably but kept asking questions as her heaving body would allow. How did it happen? The officers gave her all the information they could but stopped short of the parts that were not appropriate at the time. They didn't tell her he was traveling at over a hundred miles per hour when he crashed. They didn't tell her that the body was literally torn apart and the entire upper torso crushed and burned so that there would be no chance whatsoever that she could see him one last time. It just wasn't their place to get into that kind of detail with this poor lady. As she dealt with funeral services, she would be told about the necessity of a closed casket funeral—all in due time. It was all so very sad. And just for a minute, Officer Newell found himself feeling awfully angry at this idiot who had caused so much pain. He wasn't a kid; going that fast was a selfish and stupid thing to do. What a stupid decision!

Lynn's sister-in-law arrived and thanked the officers for being so kind and waiting. She sat beside Lynn and held her as she continued to cry. The officers walked out quietly after informing her that the Kershaw County Coroner's office would be contacting them about arrangements within the next twenty-four hours. Officer Caldwell looked at Lynn one last time and said, "We are truly sorry to have had to bring this news to you. Let your family help you get through all you have to do, and take good care of yourself." Lynn could only look up and acknowledge his kind words with a nod; she simply couldn't speak. The officers walked out to their car and drove away.

Reality

THE AFTERNOON WAS a blur of phone calls, family gatherings, and utter shock with every contact who received the news. There was not a standard way to deal with this. We live our lives wrapped up in the hope that the good things that bring us joy will simply be there every time we need them. When a reality like this rudely and unexpectedly arrives and slaps us in the face, we go into a mode that we don't even know we have. We do what must be done.

Lynn felt bad that there were some questions being asked as to the detail of the accident that she couldn't answer. She didn't remember exactly what the officers said, but what did it matter. He was gone and her life would never be the same.

Lynn's sister-in-law had stayed with her and answered the phone on Monday morning for what seemed like the millionth time. She was glad she had taken the call instead of Lynn. It was the coroner's office, and the man on the other end of the line was very cold, was very matter-of-fact, and kept referring to Pierce as "the remains." Lynn had said earlier that she wanted Lazarus Funeral Service to take care of everything for her. It was the local family-owned business, and they had been very helpful when she had lost each of her parents. She told the man on the phone that she would contact the funeral home and make the necessary arrangements.

Lynn spoke to Pierce's friend Sam on the phone for quite a while a short time after. He seemed as shocked as she was and said he would be there by late Monday afternoon. He would help in any way he could. She knew he was sincere, and she knew she would not hesitate to ask for his help. He was a good guy, and Pierce would want it that way.

The Service

It was Monday morning, and the time came to go to the funeral home and make the arrangements. Lynn knew that Pierce had a will, and she had found it. It was very clear that he had wanted to be cremated and even had noted what songs he would like to have played at the service. He had further specified that he wanted his ashes spread on the land that he had behind his house. It was all there, and she both appreciated and resented it at the same time. She wanted to be sure she had a service that would honor him and let the world know how much she loved him.

The funeral home was nice but not too over the top. She liked the understated elegance and knew Pierce would have approved. After getting up the courage to go through the front door, she and her sister-in-law were greeted by an older lady who gave her the obligatory condolences and led her to a conference room.

The conference room had a table with six leather chairs around it. There were two lamps sitting on tables at opposite ends of the room. It was a comfortable room. The lady welcomed them and assured them that they were going to be taking good care of the family. She spoke in a quiet reassuring tone.

Lynn was listening as intently as she could but found herself being taken over by her grief, and it was hard to stay focused. Suddenly, as if someone else was saying it, she heard herself say, "I want to see my husband." The statement was clear and firm, and it made Mrs. Lazarus shift a little in her seat. She reached out and took Lynn by the hand. "Dear, I understand why you feel that way, but it is simply not possible for you to do that." Lynn looked at her and very firmly said, "Why can't I?" This was a kind lady who had sat with so many people through the years and helped them to plan the process that was beyond most people's comprehension, until they were in the middle of it, but she now searched for just the right words to handle this request. "Mrs. Ellis, your husband's accident was of catastrophic nature. I think you should take some degree of comfort in the fact that he most certainly didn't suffer at all. However, the physical remains are not in a condition that would be conducive to a viewing." Lynn lowered her head and nodded. She was sobbing again, and her sister-in-law put her arm around her shoulder and said, "What else do you need from us?" The details were wrapped up in short order. It was to be a very simple memorial service, and cremation would occur on Tuesday, with the service on Wednesday afternoon.

The service went as planned, and there were many people there—more than the family could personally greet. It was very touching to see the outpouring of support, and Lynn was sure that Pierce was pleased with how it had gone. Halfway through the service, when Sam had seen that Lynn was truly struggling to make it, he had walked up behind her and gently touched her elbow. When she turned to look at him, he didn't say a word; he just smiled and handed her a loofah. They both laughed out loud, and though nearly no one else would understand, it was exactly the sort of thing that Pierce would have done and seemed to also be Sam's way of saying that she was doing well and that Pierce was proud of her. She straightened her shoulders, hugged Sam tightly, and spent the rest of the service holding the loofah in her hand.

Jeremy Richardson

JEREMY PLAYED FOOTBALL. It was the one thing that defined him. He had started playing in the eighth grade. He had a lot of natural athletic ability, but in the spring of the seventh grade, he had hit a huge growth spurt. Suddenly, he went from being the average size pudgy kid to the kid taller and stronger than the rest. He had grown to six feet tall in just a couple of months and by the end of the summer was big enough to get the attention of the middle school coach who recruited him to come out for the team.

As soon as Jeremy took the field, it was clear that he was something special. It was not just his size that made the others notice him. He could outrun, outpass, and outplay anyone his age. He had found a way to truly be a star, and he loved it. When he was on the field, Jeremy was able to leave behind his meager social status and feel special. That first year of playing football resulted in his breaking records and would lead his team to its first state championship. The coach knew about the home life and background of his star player and thanked him by giving him a used dirt bike he had fixed up in his garage. He knew Jeremy had never had anything like it before; he didn't even think the young man had owned a bicycle before. Jeremy loved it and rode it all the time. It gave him a sense of freedom and helped him feel like a normal kid.

You see Jeremy was an only child. He lived with his mom. She tried to work as best she could but struggled to hold down a job. She couldn't stand on her feet very long and was plagued with headaches so bad that she often had to stay in bed all day. Both were the result of being nearly beaten to death by Jeremy's dad when he was just four years old.

His mom's name was Kim, and she had dreams of having a happy comfortable life like most young girls do. She wanted to be a nurse. She had met Jeremy's dad David while she was a senior in high school. He was a tough guy who seemed mad at the world most of the time, but ironically, he made her feel safe. He told her he was going to be a race car driver, and she believed it was true. He seemed to have the ability to take whatever he wanted, and he had a hold on her heart that even she couldn't explain. She had lost her dad two years before in a tragic car accident and knew that he would not have approved of David at all. There was no one who was good enough for his "little princess" but especially not this certified "bad boy."

Kim's mom tried to talk to her about the likely results of this relationship and why it was such a bad idea, but she knew full well that a young girl's heart sees the world in a way that so often defies any logic until the reality of the ugly side of things comes crashing in. It was one of the most difficult things about being a parent. You can protect your child from so many of the dangers in the world, but sometimes, you simply can't protect them from the life-changing results of their own decisions.

By the time that Kim found out she was pregnant; David was already drinking heavily on a regular basis and had decided that the world was not going to allow him to become the race car driver he deserved to be. They would get married at the county courthouse before her mom even knew, and she wouldn't let David see the tears running down her face on the drive home. They moved into the two-bedroom mobile home that her family owned far out in the country just two weeks later. It was a tiny, little place, but Kim was determined to make it a home. It sat on nearly sixty acres with a long gravel driveway and the remnants of an old barn that hadn't been used in years. The land seemed even bigger than it was since it was bordered on two sides by an area that had been designated as a park although there really wasn't much there and not many people ever visited it. Still, it made for a quiet peaceful place to live, and Kim hoped that one day, she and David could build their own house there and have a happy home.

David had a job working at the local junkyard pulling parts off old cars. Customers would come in looking for a specific part and if they had the type of car the part was on; the boss would send David out to remove it, and the customer would return to pick it up. The job didn't pay much, but since he didn't have a rent payment or anything like that, he was doing alright. Plus, he was getting valuable experience that he could use to build his own race car. It was just a matter of time before he would be realizing his dream of being a driving champion. Most days, he would leave work and stop by the local quick stop for beer before going home to Kim. It became an everyday routine.

By the time their son Jeremy was born, David had already started to build his dirt track racer, and Kim had resigned herself to the fact that she would have to put her dreams of nursing school on hold until Jeremy was old enough to start school. She told herself that it was okay, and she knew her mom would help her to take care of things.

When Jeremy was just five weeks old, Kim's mom died. She had been sick for several weeks but refused to go to the doctor. When Kim couldn't reach her after several attempts one day, she called her mom's next-door neighbor and asked him to check on her. They found her dead on the kitchen floor. They told Kim she died of "natural causes" as if the natural part made it better somehow. Kim was devastated and felt very much alone.

There was a small inheritance after all the debts were settled, and Kim and David argued over the best way to handle things. Kim wanted to move out of the tiny mobile home and into her mom's house, but David insisted that he didn't want to live in the city and, besides, they could sell the house and, after taking care of the mortgage and the other bills, they would have enough to start working on building their own house on all this land. It was the perfect plan. Kim reluctantly agreed and went about settling her mom's estate.

True Reality

KIM WAS THANKFUL that her mom's car was paid off, and it was nice for Kim to have a car that was dependable. It was nine years old but in great shape and had very few miles. Maybe, things really were going to get better for her little family.

But David wasted very little time before he was working on Kim to allow him to use "just a little" of the money to buy parts for his race car—first one thing and then another. The night he came home with the extravagant trailer to show her, there was a big fight. He explained that he had to have it to haul the car around. He screamed that she just didn't understand that this was their big chance and, without the trailer, he couldn't do anything. He was going to use it to make a lot of money for their future. She knew it was useless to argue and gave in.

David began racing, and for the next three years, Kim listened to all the reasons why he wasn't winning and watched him take the money that was supposed to be for their house and spend it on his crumbling dream. The car that was Kim's only escape from the tiny mobile home began to act up while running errands in town one day. She managed to drive it to a garage to have them look it over. After a lengthy wait in the dirty waiting room, the mechanic said it was going to be $1,200 to replace the transmission, and Kim sank back in her seat as she held Jeremy on her lap. Jeremy looked up at her and smiled. He had turned four years old last week. She tried to smile back and then looked at the man and asked how long the repair would take. The man said a couple of days, so Kim called David at work to tell him what had happened and to let him know they needed a ride.

David seemed very irritated by the car news. He told Kim he would handle it. David handled all the money matters; he insisted it was his job as the man of the house to take care of their finances. He told her he got off work in a little over an hour so she could sit tight, and he would pick her up. He said he could replace the transmission himself with a used one and save a lot of money. But Kim knew it would not be a priority for him and her only means of escape for her and Jeremy would sit for days or maybe even weeks as she listened to David's excuses as to why he wasn't repairing it.

Across the street from the garage was the bank. The last time she was there was when she and David had opened the account with the money from the estate. Since she had nothing else to do, she decided to walk over.

Kim sat in the chair at the bank with Jeremy squirming on her lap. The branch manager was checking on her account for her. He came back to the desk and handed her a slip of paper telling her this was the account balance as of that day not considering any checks that hadn't been processed. She looked at the paper, and her heart sank. *How could this possibly be?* $1,980.10 was the balance. When she had settled her mom's estate, there was almost $72,000 in the account. She knew David had been using the account to buy parts for the race car, but how could it have taken so much? She felt a tear running down her face, and without saying a word, she picked up the paper and walked out of the bank.

Kim had never felt so alone in her life. She stood on the sidewalk for a few minutes, and then, she walked back into the bank and asked to close the account but was told she couldn't since both she and David's names were listed on it. She took out $1,980 and left the bank with ten cents in the account.

Kim walked across the street to the garage. She told the gentleman that she wanted to pay for the repair now and handed him the cash to do so. He happily took the money and gave her a receipt. She couldn't return his smile even though she wanted to do so. She took the receipt and went back to the grungy little seat to sit and wait for David.

The Big Race

WHEN DAVID PICKED Kim up, she said nothing to him about the account and in fact said very little at all. She knew she was in for a fight but felt numb at the moment. David was in a hurry to get home and get things ready for the big race that night. He was excitedly saying something about the big event for his class of cars and that the winner got a big payout. She wasn't even pretending to be interested this time and sat staring out the window, and Jeremy sat on her lap quietly singing the song about the wheels on the bus going round and round.

As soon as they got home, David went into the house, grabbed a six-pack of beer, and headed outside to get everything ready to leave for the race. He was checking everything out and found that he was short on fuel. He would have to pick up some on the way. There was a station where he could buy racing fuel cheaper than the fuel at the racetrack. He also remembered that he needed a few other things too so he would need to go by the ATM on the way. He felt like a kid on Christmas Eve. It all just felt right today. He had been getting faster all season and was sure that this was the night. This was the big win that would get him noticed and change everything. Now, he could pick up a few sponsors to help with the bills. He was halfway through his third beer already and feeling that the edges were a little smoother and that he was getting as primed as the bright-red number twenty-seven dirt track car that he had been working on and tweaking for more than three years now. This was going to be his night.

By the time David came bouncing inside an hour later to tell her it was time to go, she could tell he had finished most of the six-pack he had brought home. He told her they had to go because he had to stop by the ATM on the way and get some cash for the entry fee and fuel. She told him she had a headache and wouldn't be going. He was genuinely angry and hurt at the same time. He pleaded for a few minutes explaining that this was finally going to be his night, his big win. What would the guys think if she wasn't there? But he was running out of time, and she looked sick, so he gave up and walked out the door slamming it behind him. It was her loss.

Kim looked around at the tiny mobile home and realized that there would be no house to replace it, no new and better life ahead, and she began to cry. She was glad Jeremy was engrossed in the cartoon he was watching and didn't notice. For the second time on this day, she felt as if she were all alone in the world. It didn't help that there were no houses even close by, and what once seemed like such tranquility was now just emptiness, and she truly felt alone. She wanted to get a few things, get in the car, drive away, and never look back. But even that thought faded quickly as she thought of the car sitting in the garage in town. Her only means of escape now wasn't even an option. How did her life come to this? She heard the voice of her mother in her head warning her to be careful, "Seldom do we make decisions that don't carry over into the rest of our lives." Her mom was right, and that truth was yet another profound slap in the face that she would have to endure on this day. She looked down to see Jeremy had fallen asleep. Kim slid down to the floor and wrapped her arms around Jeremy tightly. She was sobbing now, and each tear that fell seemed to be tiny pieces of her hopes and dreams falling away and being replaced with the reality of her own personal prison—a prison she had built herself, day by day, never realizing that the inevitable result was the torment she felt culminating on this night. She cried to the point of exhaustion and fell asleep there in the middle of the floor with Jeremy wrapped tightly in her arms.

Race Night

DAVID WAS DRIVING toward town with the radio blaring. He was singing along with a big smile on his face, "I've got friends in low places where the whiskey drowns and the beer chases my blues away." He grabbed the beer from the cup holder, took a long drink, held up the can, and gave an imaginary toast to the air. This was a good night—his night—and it didn't even matter that Kim didn't come. By the end of this night, he was going to be a winner. Finally, he would get the respect he deserved, and it would be a stepping-stone to a whole new life. His celebratory mood would quickly change as he felt the truck start to sway erratically on the road. He knew it was probably a tire going flat, and he slammed his hand on the steering wheel. *Not now*, he thought as he felt the panic rising. He pulled to the side of the road.

It was indeed a tire going flat. It was on the left rear of the truck. He was glad it was on the truck and not the trailer. He had a spare for the truck but not the trailer, but he then realized he would have to drop the trailer to change the tire. The jack he had would not be able to lift the weight of the truck and trailer coupled together. Without another thought, he was unhooking the trailer and working to get the tire changed. It was warm outside, and he was already sweating. He was working quickly when he was startled by a voice, "Having some trouble?" It was a highway patrolman—the last thing he needed. He knew he had to stay calm and as far away from the police officer as he could. He felt a wave of panic as he thought about the beer cans in the floorboard of the truck and the one unopened beer on the front seat. The rest was in a cooler inside the trailer, but there was enough in the cab of the truck to cause a whole lot of trouble.

The police officer was in the last hour of a long shift. He just wanted to see if he could help. He walked up to the man working feverishly to change a flat tire. "Evening, sir. You got everything you need to get her changed?" Without looking up, David said in his friendliest voice, "Yes, sir, just trying to get this done and get to the track, already running late. It's always something, right? The officer stood behind him shining his flashlight where David was feverishly working. He replied, "Sure is, especially if you're in a hurry." David saw the officer shift a little as if to move toward the cab of the truck, and he quickly said, "That flashlight is a big help. I really appreciate your stopping. I will be finished here in just a minute or two." It worked. The officer stood behind him and shined the flashlight on the center of the tire as David was putting the lug nuts on. David could hear a car approaching, and as it got closer, it was apparent it was speeding. It passed them in a blur, and the officer said very quickly, "You got this?" David said, "Sure, you go ahead." And just like that, the officer was gone, and David smiled as he tightened the last lug nut. He finished up quickly and put everything away, hooked the trailer back up, and jumped in the front seat. "Just a speed bump," he said out loud and started down the road.

About a mile from town David came to the bank with the ATM. He inserted the card, put in his code, and entered a withdrawal amount of $160. That should cover it for tonight. He was smiling and feeling the excitement building again as he thought about getting to the track just three miles away. And then, he noticed the screen had just two words, Transaction Denied. For the second time tonight, David pounded his hand on the steering wheel and quickly tried to go over in his head the last amount shown on the receipt last week when he had taken money out. *Wasn't it nearly $2000?* The panic was rising, and he quickly entered the numbers again and tried $100, but the result was the same. He slammed the dashboard and pressed the key to show him the account balance. It came back as

$0.10. *What!* David's head was spinning, *How could this be?* Had he forgotten something? He couldn't check with the bank since it was closed. There was a car behind him, so he pulled slowly away and started toward the track. He fished in his pockets for every dollar, and he counted out enough to get in but only $22 for fuel. It's not enough. Maybe, one of the guys would be kind enough to let him borrow a little. He had to try.

When he got to the track, the other cars were already out warming up so he hurried to find a spot. David was hustling to get the car out of the trailer and looking around the crowd for someone who he could ask for either a little cash or to see if they were carrying extra fuel. He started the car and checked the fuel gauge. With what was already in the tank and the cash he had, he knew he would have a little more than three-quarters of a tank. He could only hope to run the race if he didn't run any warm-up laps at all. He decided to do that rather than beg the other drivers for help. He felt a sense of guarded relief and went about putting on his fire suit.

The race for David's class of cars, the main event, was announced, and the cars began to move to line up. Tonight's lineup was based on points from the finishes during the season, and David was in a solid fourth place slot that gave him a great position. He felt the combination of adrenaline and alcohol as he moved around the track. This was going to be his night. He had polished off two more beers waiting for the race to start and had two six-packs in the cooler waiting for the victory celebration.

The race started, and before the second lap was completed, there was a wreck coming out of turn two. It would prove to be a precursor for the entire event. There was one wreck after another with long delays to clean up and more caution laps than racing laps. It was annoying to all the drivers, but for David, it was a potential disaster as he watched his fuel gauge move down. The race was supposed to be fifty laps, and they had only completed twenty.

Now, there were only nine of the twenty-four cars left in the race, and David was in the second position. They managed to run eighteen laps before one of the cars lost control and ran into the wall. They cleared the car quickly.

During the next ten laps, David was on the bumper of the lead car, and the crowd was on their feet. As he came out of turn two, the car ahead of him hesitated just slightly, and David moved past him into the lead. He was as excited as he had ever been. He was in the lead, and when he crossed the line, there would only be two laps to run. Now, he just had to be smart and keep the lead. As he came out of turn three, he saw the yellow caution lights come on. One of the cars had a tire going down and was limping slowly to get off the track when another had hit it hard and slammed it up against the wall pushing the front end up so that it was perched on the wall and couldn't move. It took several long caution laps to remove the car, and David was very nervous now as he watched his gas gauge hanging precariously close to empty. But there were just two laps to go, and it was done. He was going to be in the winner's circle where he belonged.

The wrecked car was finally cleared, and as David crossed the line under the green flag, he felt a sickening shutter. The engine smoothed out for a few seconds and then shuttered again before going silent. David slammed his hand hard on the steering wheel again and again as he struggled to move the car to the inside of the track. He saw the yellow lights come on and just like that it was over. He was out of gas just two laps from his big victory. The other cars rolled past him, and the tow truck came out to push him to the infield and back to the spot where his trailer sat. The decision not to get more fuel turned out to be a very bad one indeed.

David got out of his car and threw his helmet. *How could this have happened?* He was so close. He went to the cooler and grabbed a beer. It would be the first of four before he got help from a couple of guys next to him to push the car on to the trailer. He would grab the rest and put them in the cab of the truck before leaving. He didn't want to talk to anyone; he just wanted to get out of there.

He headed home running through the night's events in his head, and he kept coming back to the money. Where had it gone? How could he have lost track of it that badly?

When he pulled up in front of the little mobile home, he turned off the truck and just sat there. He finished off three more beers sitting there alone in the quiet darkness.

Kim had fallen asleep with Jeremy sitting on her lap, but she woke up when David pulled up outside. She felt a wave of dread come over her as she thought about David confronting her over the money that he surely had found out she had taken when he went to the ATM. But she had questions for him too. How could he have been so selfish and used all the money that was really hers, to begin with? How could he care so little about her and his own little boy? He would be mad, but she had a right to have some answers, and she intended to get some. She took Jeremy to his room, took her time to tuck him in, and came back out. She looked out the window and saw David still sitting there in the truck. After a few very long minutes, she made the decision to go outside. It was better to have the argument that was surely coming outside so that they wouldn't wake up Jeremy. Besides, David had quite a temper and would occasionally throw things and get very loud when he was extremely angry. And she knew he would certainly be upset tonight but had no way of knowing just how badly his night had gone.

Kim stepped out of the door and walked up to the truck. David was sitting there staring straight ahead. There was an awkward silence, and then, David began to speak in that slurred rapid way that he did when he had been drinking way too much. He was saying that he had been doing so well and telling her the whole story when Kim blurted out that she had to take the money and that she wasn't sorry that she did.

In David's alcohol-altered state, it took a couple of minutes to register, but then, he realized what she had said. He felt the rage building up inside him as Kim went on about how stupid he was to waste so much money! She cried as she said that that money was for their future, but despite the tears, there was a solid resolve in her voice, and she wasn't backing down. David opened the truck door and got out. He was wavering from the now overwhelming combination of rage and alcohol. David lost all control. He hit her with the back of his hand and knocked her to the ground. She kicked at him and told him he was a worthless disgusting drunk. When she added that he was never going to be anything but a loser, he felt like his head would explode, and he began to kick her repeatedly. He was in a blind fit of rage and stopped only when he realized there was blood pouring out of the side of Kim's head. She had fallen against a rock and had opened a large gash in her right temple. She was lying motionless on the ground, and the rage now turned to panic.

After trying to revive her for a few short seconds, he went inside and dialed 911. The first to arrive on the scene was the local first responders from the volunteer fire department. It was very apparent that the lady clinging to life hadn't fallen as the obviously inebriated man had explained. They kept an eye on him as they tended to her as best as they could while they waited for the ambulance to arrive. One of them put in a call to the local sheriff to send a car out.

When the deputy sheriff arrived, he quickly accessed the situation and put David in handcuffs placing him in the back of the car. David looked out the window at the little mobile home and the ambulance, and he knew things were bad but didn't know the decisions he had made this night would keep him from seeing any of it, including his son, for many years.

After a lot of hard work on the part of the DA's office, David was convicted of several charges including attempted murder. He was sentenced to twenty years. It would be twelve years before he would be eligible for parole.

Jeremy would spend nearly four months in foster care while his mom was in the hospital recovering and for the few weeks when she had returned home but was too weak to care for him. Her injuries had taken her to the brink of death. The second night she was in the hospital had been the worst when the swelling of her brain had caused her body to begin to shut down. The doctors called it a miracle that she survived, and one commented that she seemed to choose to live. But her survival was one that would not be without struggles that went far beyond her time in the hospital and the grueling weeks in rehabilitation but would indeed last the rest of her life.

The day that Kim was well enough to have Jeremy come home was the first time she had allowed herself to genuinely smile in nearly four months. Kim knew that she had a difficult road ahead of her in so many ways, but she would find a way to make her life and more importantly Jeremy's life as good as she possibly could. She had felt alone in the past, but she now had to deal with the fact that her life and her family consisted of just her and Jeremy.

She relied on assistance from the state and felt ashamed at first. She really wanted to work, but the severe debilitating headaches that the doctors couldn't help her with totally overwhelmed her at times. Twice, she had tried to work. She had found a job as a waitress and did okay for a few weeks, until the day the owner of the restaurant watched as she dropped a whole tray full of food, when the headache she had tried to work through became too much and had taken over her body. The lady in booth number three, who had been the unfortunate victim of all that was on the tray, was less than understanding. Her boss felt he had no choice but to let Kim go.

Her second job lasted less than two weeks when she called in for a third day, out of eight, crying, and said the pain she was in was just too much. It was not that great a job, but she so wanted to feel like she was doing something to take care of herself. It was the last time she would try to work for many years to come.

Jeremy's Childhood

As Jeremy grew, the woods and fields around him became more and more important. His mom was often sick, so he found it best to find ways to spend his time away from the little mobile home allowing her to rest.

He loved being outdoors and knew every inch of the land that surrounded him. There was a large tract of public land on one side of their property that made it seem as if it went on forever.

When Jeremy was twelve years old, he found a rifle in the back of the closet in the kitchen. He was trembling as he held it in his hands. His mother was asleep, so he quietly took it outside to look it over. It looked old but seemed to work. He crept back inside and looked in the closet to see if there were any bullets to be found there. There in a small wooden case he found several boxes of ammunition. He tried to lift the box very carefully so that he wouldn't make any noise. He successfully lifted it from its resting place and went back outside.

Once outside, Jeremy ran with the rifle and the box of bullets. He ran deep into the woods and found a spot in some rocks where there was a small natural cave. He examined every inch of the rifle and pulled back the bolt revealing the groove where the bullet sat before being moved forward and into position. He moved the bolt up and back into place. He pulled the trigger just slightly, and the hammer released making a sharp snapping sound. Jeremy smiled. For some reason, this rifle gave him a feeling of power that he had never felt before. He took one of the boxes of bullets from the wooden case and headed even deeper into the woods. When he felt sure neither his mom nor anyone else would be able to hear the gun, he stopped and carefully loaded a bullet into the rifle. Though he wasn't quite sure he was doing it right, his trembling hand pushed the bolt forward that moved the bullet into place. The old rifle had a small button with a red dot on it, but it was loose and fell forward when the bolt was pushed into position. As he looked down at it, his finger rested on the trigger, and even the very slight pressure he exerted on it caused the rifle to fire, and the startled Jeremy dropped it and jumped straight up. He immediately went from shocked disbelief to a broad smile and could not pick it up fast enough as he looked wildly around to see if anyone was in the area. It had fallen on a bed of thick leaves and had not been damaged at all so Jeremy brushed it off and held it up again examining all the working parts of his newfound treasure. The first time he fired it, he was surprised at how loud it was, and yet, it was a great feeling, just the same. He spent the next couple of hours shooting the rifle. It was a good day.

Later, he returned home and hid the rifle and remaining bullets in the old barn.

Over the next few months, he would take the gun out and fire it a few times until the day there were only three bullets left. He decided that he had better keep them, just in case. After all, he was the man of the house now and needed to be able to protect his mom.

When Jeremy wasn't in school, he spent most of his time alone. He often wished that there were other kids around to hang out with, but there were only a couple of houses nearby, and no kids lived in either of them. He wondered sometimes why his parents had made the choice to live so far away from everything and wondered what it might be like to be able to spend time with his father in the way that other kids talked about it at school or even with his mom if she were not so sick most of the time.

By the time Jeremy had turned sixteen years old, there wasn't any area in the land that surrounded the tiny mobile home that he hadn't explored. It was a solitary life in many ways, but he found himself lost in thought about the upcoming football season and his chance to shine again. It was the first week of July, and he was already looking forward to the team's first official meeting and practice. Already, he was going to the weight room three times a week to work out. One of the guys picked him up on the way. Rain or shine, Jeremy always walked to the end of the driveway and out to the main road and was picked up there. He avoided the embarrassment of having anyone see the tiny rusted mobile home where he lived. He would always leave very early, arriving at the end of the road as much as an hour before the agreed time. But he dreamed of the day that he would live in a much nicer place and hoped that what the coach had told him about playing hard and working to always get better would indeed pay off one day and take him there.

The Call

IT WAS MORNING on what appeared to be another hot day in this second week of July. Jeremy was up early and hoping to spend some time working on changing the tire on his motorcycle. It had taken him several weeks to gather the money and find a used tire that would fit. He missed having the bike to ride and took good care of it. It was too small for him now that he had grown so much, but he still loved the feeling of freedom that he had when he was on it. He had worked out a deal with the old man down the street to do chores occasionally in trade for a few dollars for gas and parts for his bike.

He was eating cereal and watching his mom try to have a conversation with him about his plans for the day. She looked very old now, and he tried to remember the last time he had seen her have a genuine smile on her face. It startled them both when the phone rang. They didn't get many calls. His mom picked up the phone and said, "Hello." She said nothing for several minutes, but Jeremy could tell by the look on her face that this was not a friendly call. There was a mixture of fear and something else, and she listened intently.

The voice on the other end of the phone was David—the man who had gone into a fit of drunken rage and forever changed her life, the man who had taken away her dreams and hopes and those of the only real love she had ever known, her son Jeremy. David had been released on parole the day before and was going on and on about how he had already found a job and was a totally different man and most of all just how sorry he was about everything. He explained that the counseling he had received during his time in prison had helped him see and understand the mistakes he had made. When he started talking about how great it was to be free again and working on a new future, Kim started to cry and scream at the same time. She found a strength she hadn't felt in years. She screamed at David, "What about my life? What about the hell that I live through every single day just trying to survive? You call here telling me about your hope for the future and expect me to be glad to hear from you?" She went on to chronicle the pain and sorrow his decision on that terrible night had brought down on both her and Jeremy. And then, she was quietly sobbing as she still held the phone to her ear. She said, "I don't want to see you, and I don't care what the court says about a visitation to see Jeremy, supervised or not. I simply don't want you here and just want to be left alone." She listened again for some time as Jeremy sat staring at her and feeling frozen by all that he had heard. He wanted to go to his mom and hug her in an attempt to comfort her but could not move.

As she continued to listen, her face seemed to soften some, and she said, "I'm sorry, but I just don't know, and I will think about it. I have to go now because I feel a major migraine coming on and I have to lie down." She hung up the phone. She knew Jeremy was smart enough to understand what was going on. She walked over to him, hugged him very tightly, and said, "Everything will be okay. I have to go lie down now but just know that I will protect you." Jeremy felt a tear escaping from his own eye but quickly wiped it away so his mom would not see it when she released her embrace. He said to his mom, "I won't let anything happen to you." It was not just a hollow statement. For Jeremy, it was a real concrete declaration that he would honor no matter what happened.

She went to the tiny bedroom and shut the door. Jeremy sat quietly for a few minutes and then went outside to work on the motorcycle tire. After about an hour, he was trying to remove the bolt holding the right side of the tire, and as he put all his substantial strength into the effort, the stud broke off and fell to the ground. It was an older bike, and the strain of years of riding, especially by a kid who had outgrown the bike a couple of years ago, had taken its toll. He threw the wrench down, cursed under his breath, and left the mess there. Jeremy went inside to wash up and take the walk down to the end of the long road to meet his ride for his Saturday work-out. Before he left, he went to the barn and grabbed the old rifle. He looked at it intently, and for the first time, it felt necessary. He needed it to protect his mom. It was no longer just a fun way to pass the time, it was vital, and having it gave him a sense of comfort. It felt heavier, and for the first time, he looked at it as a real weapon. While his mom stayed locked away in her room, he quietly took it inside and very carefully leaned into the corner of the closet in his room.

David Comes Home

It was morning, and Kim awoke to discover the small window-unit air conditioner that was woefully inadequate for the job of cooling the metal mobile home on days that neared a hundred degrees had stopped working sometime during the night. It was very warm in the tiny mobile home and soon would be nearly unbearable if the ninety-four-degree forecast was indeed correct. Once again, she found herself wishing that there were shade trees close enough to give some relief, but of course, that was a wasted thought—one that could be added to the barrel of wishes that seemed to be most of her thoughts on days like this. She got up and made coffee and opened as many windows as she could. She knew there was little she could do to remedy the situation and find someone who might be able to repair the air conditioner since it was Sunday. And did anyone even repair old window units? It was just one more hurdle to overcome. They seemed to never end.

She was on her second cup of coffee when she heard the faint sound of a car approaching. Kim pulled back the faded curtain and saw an older model vehicle that she did not recognize turn off the road and start down the gravel driveway. She was frozen, and even in the increasing swelter of the day, she felt a chill creep slowly from the back of her neck to the base of her spine. As the car got close enough for her to see inside, an audible gasp escaped from her mouth. Even though it had been years since she saw his face, she was stunned by the realization that it was David in the car.

She gathered all the strength and resolve that her tiny fragile body could muster and stepped out the door onto the little platform that served as a porch. She trembled as she waited for him to get out of the car. She was trying intently to calm and steady herself but felt a little dizzy.

David managed a smile as he got out. He hoped it would help put Kim at ease, and he stopped and looked up at the lady he once knew as the love of his life and his intended lifelong companion and said, "Hi, Kim." He was a little shocked at how thin and frail she appeared. Had he passed her on the street, he wasn't even sure he would have recognized her.

There was an awkward silence, and then, with power in her voice and very obvious resolve, Kim said loudly, "David, don't come any closer. You need to leave. It is just not a good idea for you to be here. I have not had a chance to talk to Jeremy, and you are just showing up here like this? It is totally unacceptable! We really just don't want or need you here."

Inside his tiny bedroom, Jeremy was waking up. Even though he was wearing only a pair of gym shorts, he was sweating and very uncomfortable. In the fog between being awake and asleep, he thought he heard voices, and it did not sound like the little television. As he drifted in and out of consciousness, he was suddenly jolted awake by the shrill sound of his mother's voice saying, "Just leave! You are not welcome here, not now, not ever!" He sat up in bed and looked out the window at the man he did not recognize but knew was his own father. He leaped to his feet and made the decision that he would protect his mom and force this man he did not know, but ironically understood to be his father, to leave with hopes he would never return. Jeremy quickly grabbed the rifle from the corner of his closet and put a bullet in it. His hands were shaking so that it took several attempts to get the bullet into the chamber. Twice, he dropped it, and he cursed out loud as sweat dripped from his nose. As soon as it was in place, he ran for the front door.

Jeremy opened the door just enough to get his toned and slender frame quickly past his mother. He leveled the rifle at the man he knew was his father but was just a dangerous stranger now looking wide-eyed at him and said, "My mom said she didn't want you here. Leave now!"

Kim was shocked by the sight and screamed, "Jeremy, please put that down and go back inside. I can handle this." But Jeremy was looking only at David, and he was shaking all over with a combination of resolve and anger as he kept the old rifle aimed carefully. The need to be the protector of the one person who had shown him unconditional love his whole life was too strong to allow him to back down.

David gave Jeremy a half-smile and said, "Now, son, you know you are not going to hurt me or anyone else with that old rifle of mine. Why heck, I would be surprised if it will even fire at all. Please just put that down, and we can all talk. I just wanted to see you, son, and tell you how sorry I am about how everything happened. I am a changed man, Jeremy, and son, I want to prove that to you and to your mom as well." With an attempt to be charming and diffuse the situation, David added with a smile, "I am so surprised at how big you are and just want to spend a little time with you." Jeremy felt a tear running down his cheek, and he pushed the safety of the rifle to the fire position, and it made a loud undeniable click that hung in the hot air for a moment. He pointed it directly at David's head. This time in a low, determined, and guttural tone, Jeremy said, "Don't call me son, and do as my mom asked you. Get back in your car and don't ever come back."

David held up both hands in a gesture of compliance and looked at Kim and said, "Can't you talk to him and set things, right?" At that moment, the emotion and uncertainty of the moment coupled with the rising fury Jeremy was experiencing caused the young man to shake even more, and his finger applied just slightly more pressure to the trigger, and the gun fired, and the world forever changed.

The bullet entered David's right eye, and with shock and disbelief, he immediately clasped his hand over it and crumpled to his knees. All three of them were frozen in time as the stark reality of what had just happened sank in. The rifle was a twenty-two caliber so the velocity of the bullet was not enough to penetrate and pass through the skull, so it simply bounced around inside and killed David almost immediately. He dropped face first into the dirt still clasping his own eye.

Both Kim and Jeremy looked on in horror and disbelief as David lay on the ground twitching and trying to utter some sound. Blood poured from his hand, and in the greatest of ironies, he fell in the same spot where Kim had bled on that fateful night years before. He suddenly stopped moving.

Jeremy spun around and looked at Kim still standing directly behind him; with both horror and disbelief in his eyes, he uttered, "I'm sorry, Mom." Wearing no shoes and only his gym shorts, he ran across the field and into the woods, still carrying the rifle in his hand. Kim collapsed onto the step and tried to take in what had just happened. She was so stunned that she could neither speak nor move.

Jeremy ran swiftly despite the fact that he was wearing no shoes. He had to get away as quickly as possible and as far away as he could. No one, especially the police, would understand that it was an accident. He just kept running until he came to the gravel parking area for the woods he knew so well and for what others called Forty Acre Rock. As he started to run along the edge of the lot, he saw a man that had gotten off his motorcycle and was standing awkwardly with one of his boots off and was pouring water on his foot. Jeremy saw that there were no other cars in the parking lot. He suddenly made the decision that this motorcycle was his means to get far away from here very quickly.

For the second time this morning, he raised the rifle and ran toward the man who was too preoccupied to notice him. Jeremy startled the man when he said, "Mister, I am really sorry, and I really don't want to hurt you, but I have to take your motorcycle." The man was stunned by the sudden realization that a young man was right beside him and that he was looking down the barrel of a rifle. He held up his hands in a show of compliance and said, "Hold on now. What is this about? Just put the gun down. Don't do something you are going to regret, son."

The young man standing before him was clearly shaking and looked very serious. He looked overwhelmingly scared and was visibly unstable. But the gentleman standing by his motorcycle in a vulnerable position, with his boot removed, hoped he could find out what the problem was and stop this from going any further. Before he could utter another word and begin to reason with the young man, the rifle was moved even closer to his head, and he was told to move, and a gesture was made toward the path at the edge of the parking lot. He reluctantly moved in that direction. "I'm not sure what has happened this morning to you, but maybe, I can help you out." Jeremy said, "Please, mister. Just keep moving, and I will not have to hurt you. I didn't want anyone to get hurt, but this is the way it must be now. Please just don't talk anymore." Jeremy saw the rolls of duct tape and the bungee cords that were at the top of the open saddlebag and grabbed them. He told the man to grab the boot that he had removed, and they hurriedly walked about three hundred yards down the wooded path until Jeremy said, "There, on the left, up the side of the hill between those rocks, that's where we are going." They climbed the hill and walked between two exceptionally large boulders. These rocks were both bigger than a school bus, and Jeremy told the man to walk behind the one to his left. He then said, "I hate to do this, sir, but I am going to have to trade clothes with you." The man looked at Jeremy with some disbelief but could see he had better comply with the request. Jeremy saw a kind softness in his eyes, and it made all he was doing even harder. But in short order, Jeremy was wearing the man's shirt and pants and the boots he had told the man to grab before leaving the parking area. The unfortunate man now found himself wearing only Jeremy's gym shorts. There were several points in the process where he felt like he might have been able to overpower Jeremy and could have taken the gun from him, but even now, he felt like he could reason with this young man and help him to see that his actions were leading him farther down a road that could only mean deep trouble for him. Jeremy cinched up the belt as tightly as he could to keep the pants up. He reached into the back pocket of the pants and pulled out the wallet. He looked at the driver's license of Mr. Pierce Ellis and noted there were cash and some credit cards. He also found the keys in the front pocket, one of which would have to be the motorcycle key. He looked down at the keys but saw none that seemed to be for the motorcycle. He asked Pierce, "Where is the key to the bike?" Pierce explained that the bike didn't have a key, it would start as soon as you were close enough to it with the round key fob that said Indian on it. The young man seemed hesitant to believe him but put the assorted keys back in his pocket.

Jeremy told Pierce to sit down at the base of a small tree that was about six inches in diameter. The tree was far enough behind the rock to be hidden from anyone who might be on the path below. When Pierce reluctantly complied, Jeremy handed him the first roll of duct tape and said, "Wind it around your ankles until I tell you to stop." Pierce looked up at him and said, "Look, just take the bike, and go, but you don't have to do all this." But Jeremy looked to be on the verge of panic and still shaking. He loudly screamed, "Please just do it!" Pierce wrapped the tape tightly around his ankles multiple times, and finally, Jeremy said, "Okay, that's enough. Now, hand the tape to me and put your hands behind your back on either side of the tree." Pierce thought for a moment as he hesitated about trying to grab the gun from the young man, but after a moment's hesitation, he complied. Jeremy again apologized, and as he wound the tape tightly again and again around the man's wrists, he explained that he was heading north and, in a couple of hours when he was far enough away, he would call the police and let them know where to find Pierce. The troubled young man certainly sounded sincere. He continued to wind the tape around Pierce's wrists until the entire roll was gone. He then stood up and said, "For what it's worth, mister, I am really sorry about all of this, but you will be just fine." He then used the bungee cords to further bind Pierce in place. As he turned to leave, he heard voices in the parking lot and felt the panic rise. He turned quickly and used the second roll of tape to cover Pierce's mouth by applying it around his head and over his mouth numerous times. He sat with his heart pounding as he heard the people on the path walk by just below where they were hidden behind the rocks.

When he was sure they were gone, he bolted, leaving Pierce without looking back.

Jeremy ran halfway down the path back toward the gravel lot, and then, as an afterthought, he ran back past the rocks where the man was now bound. He looked up to be sure that no one was on the path and could see him. Once he had confirmed that the man was indeed out of sight, he ran until he got to a pond that lies about 300 yards past the rocks. With all the strength he could muster, he threw the rifle into the lake. It really wasn't much use anyway since the only bullet that had been in it was fired earlier, and he was relieved that the man had complied with his demands. The empty gun had done what he hoped it would. And for an instant, he stopped cold as he could see the gun going off earlier and the bullet striking the man who felt like a stranger but that he knew to be his father. He did not mean for that to happen at all. He only wanted him to leave and to protect his mom. Nothing would ever be the same again, and he knew it. He turned and ran back to the parking lot.

Jeremy emerged out of the woods and ran to the motorcycle. He was relieved to see only one car in the lot that would have been the vehicle of those who had passed by earlier. He knew they were likely to be walking the trails for quite some time. His heart pounded, and the sweat was oozing out of every pore as he ran to the motorcycle. Jeremy quickly closed the saddlebags and put on the helmet that was too large but would have to do. He snugged it as tightly as he could with the chinstrap. When he got on the bike, he was surprised by how heavy it felt. He looked it over quickly and pushed the button the man had said would start the bike. It started, and he was surprised by how loud it was. Without hesitation, he pushed the bike backward and was very unsteady in the gravel and with the unfamiliar weight. When he felt like he had backed up far enough to be able to leave the lot, Jeremy pushed down on the gear lever with his foot to put the bike in gear and released the clutch slowly. It lurched forward, and Jeremy pulled out of the parking lot and on to the road. It was so much bigger than the little trail bike he had ridden for years, and yet, it was similar enough that he could figure it out. He was a bit wobbly at first, but as soon as he started to roll a bit faster, it felt steady and powerful.

He had told the man he was heading north intentionally because he was going to head south. He had traveled very little during his life but knew a few of the roads from his bus travel to football games. He would head toward Camden and then just keep going south until he got to Florida before ditching the bike. He had seen pictures of Florida, and it looked like as good a place as any to go at this point. Maybe, he could find a way to survive there without telling people his real name. He was all alone now and needed to get used to the idea. He had to put away the thoughts of his mom right now and move quickly. This was about survival now.

The bike was powerful, and he had to slow himself down several times as he realized he was speeding and could not risk any attention or of course getting stopped by an alert patrol officer. He felt a sense of panic as he noticed the fuel light glowing. He would have to stop and get gas.

Jeremy was a little shaky as he pulled into a gas station that was not far down the road. Luckily, there was no one in the parking lot on this Sunday morning. He managed to maneuver the bike close to the gas pump and turned it off. He found the credit cards in the wallet and inserted one into the pump. He held his breath as it read authorizing and then exhaled when it gave him the signal to begin fueling. Jeremy quickly filled the tank and got back on the bike.

He was very relieved when he was able to pull out of the parking lot and get back on the road.

Jeremy's mind was racing as he tried to comprehend all that had happened. How had things spiraled so out of control? He wondered if the police were already there. But he knew that if they were, they would be looking for him in the woods, and he should have some time before they discovered the man behind the rocks. *Funny, he seemed like a nice guy*, and Jeremy felt bad about leaving him there.

Peace for Kim

BACK ON THE steps of the little mobile home, Kim sat in utter shock and panic. She was completely overwhelmed by the events and as she watched Jeremy disappear into the woods and looked on in horror at David's lifeless body lying just feet from her in a pool of blood. She felt a warm sensation in her head, and then, everything went black. The massive stroke would take her life very quickly, and her battered body would fall crumpled on the steps as her life slipped away. Kim's suffering was finally over. It would be several days before Jeremy's football coach would come to check on him and find the horrific aftermath of the morning, both dead bodies, and would notify authorities.

Jeremy was riding slowly through the mostly empty streets of the town of Camden when he noticed a police car on the side of the road. It was sitting in the parking lot of a small restaurant. He felt the panic rise in him as the police car pulled into the road and was now following him. Jeremy could feel his whole body shaking, and he looked down at the speedometer to be sure he was not speeding. He looked quickly in the mirror and noticed the young officer holding the mic from the radio. He was speaking to someone, and Jeremy now felt the sense of real panic taking him over. *Was the officer calling in the tag? Was it possible that the people on the trail had somehow found the man and had already notified the police?* He further panicked when he realized the stoplight ahead was yellow and about to turn red. He brought the bike to a smooth stop and sat at the stoplight with his heart pounding and without moving his head at all. He watched the officer in the mirror as he continued to talk to someone on the radio. He could feel his whole body shaking and was afraid he would drop the motorcycle. Jeremy expected the lights on the police car to come on at any moment. Just as he pulled away when the light turned green, he felt a buzzing in his pocket and realized it was a cell phone. The officer was again talking with someone, and the combination of it all caused his panic to rise past his ability to contain it, and he took off to get away before the cop behind him had time to react. In no time at all, he was traveling at over a hundred miles per hour. He looked at the on-ramp for the interstate, and as he started to take it, he noticed a patrol car at the top of the ramp with its lights flashing so he made a last-second decision to swerve back on to the highway, and just for a second, he felt as if he was riding on ice. And then, in an instant, the bike was out of control as it veered off the side of the road bouncing off the guardrail and slamming into the concrete support of the overpass. Jeremy's solitary life ended in much the same way he had spent so many days, alone and unknown.

Survival

PIERCE WAS VERY uncomfortable and decided to once again see if he could free his hands from the tape. He had tried several times before with no success, but now, as he was perspiring more, he thought he may have a better chance. As he moved his right arm as hard as he could, he felt his shoulder slip out of its joint dislocating it, and the pain was excruciating. He had injured it a few years before in an accident at a friend's house when he stopped by and was asked to help put a large bay window in place. It had fallen on him as the less than intellectually gifted individual inside had failed to hold it in place as he tapped it to try to adjust the way it sat in the frame. It had taken six of them to lift it into place, and he had no hopes of holding it up once it began to fall. It had been extremely painful for weeks afterward and still caused him trouble periodically. He really should have sued them and had it properly taken care of, but it wasn't his nature to do such things. He had heard that once you were injured in that way, it was more likely to occur again. And for the second time today, the thought that "no good deed goes unpunished" ran through his mind. He was squirming and trying to move to pop it back in place as he had before, but his range of movement was not enough to successfully get it back in the proper position. He was sweating profusely from a combination of the now rising temperature and the overwhelming pain and had to force himself to stop moving and trying and calm down. Certainly, there would be someone along soon to set him free. It had been nearly two hours since the young man had left him and told Pierce he would notify authorities where he could be found. For Pierce, it seemed to have been much longer. And even after all that happened, Pierce believed that there was something very fragile and genuinely sorry in his tone. He didn't believe the young man was a bad person and would do as he said he would. But it was beyond uncomfortable now, and the relief could not come soon enough.

The next few hours were nearly unbearable, and Pierce had thought he had heard voices on the path below only once. He had tried very hard to make noise so they might hear him but could only manage some muffled grunts that he knew had very little chance of being heard.

The pain in his shoulder had dulled, and he didn't dare try to move again. It was now a mental game of trying to keep his mind calm with the hope that at any moment someone would arrive and this would be over.

Pierce thought of Lynn and wondered what she was doing. He was glad that she was unaware of this whole crazy day and all that had happened. He really was going to have quite a story to tell her this evening.

The time moved very slowly, but eventually, it was midafternoon and very hot. Pierce had been thirsty for some time now, but it was becoming difficult to swallow, and the thought of his pouring the bottles of water on his legs earlier was torture. It was increasingly difficult to breath as the temperature rose and his mouth was completely covered. He tried to wiggle his mouth with hopes that the combination of movement and perspiration would force the tape to drop so he could breathe easier and call for help when he heard someone below on the path. But he could not get the tape to budge. There were just too many layers wrapped tightly around the entire lower half of his face.

And now, it came to the point that he had to ask, *Why? How did he get here, and what could possibly have driven a young man who didn't seem to be a typical thug to such desperate measures? Why was he running through the woods clad only in gym shorts, with no shoes, and carrying a rifle?* But then again, it was all part of that mystery that was simply life. So many times, Pierce had been amazed and confused by the actions of people, even those that he thought he knew well. But through time, he arrived at the conclusion that he had created a lot of misery for himself when he had spent so much time hoping that the people, especially those he truly cared about, would somehow be different than they naturally were. This young man may have been acting in a way that was just a reflection of his personality that had been formed through both nature and nurture or maybe the lack of it. Though it was hard to comprehend, there are those who simply take. There are some who are thankful for all that is done for them and others who quickly forget. Some will work hard and want only what they have earned, and yet, there are individuals who feel as if they are owed what others have regardless of their own personal efforts. It is quite liberating when you finally realize that you need to accept people as they are and not as you would like them to be. Pierce had come to the inevitable conclusion that you will be disappointed much less and have a lot more time and resources to spend on the deserving aspects of your life when that realization to eliminate pre-conceived expectations becomes one of the cornerstones of your own personal philosophy.

And now, as he sat, random thoughts came. It occurred to him that a child's self-esteem has been the goal of most parents for the past couple of generations. Apparently, it is evident that it is time to return to lessons of gratitude, self-reliance, humility, and the idea that the world is not here for you but you are here to find your place in the world. Maybe, that young man's family should have worked harder on that for him, and they would in turn be working on his place in society for the rest of us. But mostly right now, he was just thirsty and thinking about how great it was going to be to simply stand up.

As the day wore on, Pierce became aware that he was no longer sweating even though the temperature had to be in the middle nineties. He knew he was becoming seriously dehydrated, and it was far beyond just being thirsty now. He was hungry too since he hadn't eaten all day, but the thirst was the most overwhelming feeling. Where was his help? Somebody, anybody!

Of course, Pierce had no way of knowing all the tragic events that had taken place and the fact that even as he sat here in misery, there was not a person alive who knew where he was and could help him.

Desperation

PIERCE FELT VERY dizzy and disoriented at times. It was now very late afternoon. He heard the leaves rustling and watched as a large black snake with a ring around its neck slithered past his foot. Although he recognized it as a nonpoisonous king snake, it was very unnerving just the same, and his heart was racing. Long after it was out of sight, his heart was still pounding in his head. The snake was no longer the reason. It was the next symptom of the dehydration that was taking over his body. He tried calming himself and could do nothing to control it. Pierce needed water soon.

He watched as the sun went down and got angry all over again when the idea of spending the night here in the woods started to become a possibility. *Why hadn't the kid made the call?* He would not allow himself to believe that he was not going to contact the police and let them know he was there. As the darkness began to chase away the remnants of the sunlight, Pierce was drifting from consciousness and then was out.

Pierce woke in the middle of the night to the pounding of his heart and the disturbing reality of where he was and his now searing thirst. A sense of panic rose in him, and he began to flail about in an effort to be free, but moving his now severely swollen shoulder was excruciating. The maddening pounding of his heart in his head was deafening and utter torture, and for the first time, Pierce allowed himself to wonder if he would die here alone in these woods. After a short period, he passed out again.

Pierce was aware of the silence around him as he awakened in the dim light of the morning. In addition to the pain, he was cold and shivering. The damp night air and the fact that he was clad only in gym shorts were just some more difficulty that was added to his struggle. As he opened his eyes, he saw two large deer just on the top of the ridge. Even through the fog of all he was enduring, he was aware of just how beautiful they were.

Pierce had grown up around guns and hunting. He allowed his mind to drift back to the fall morning which became one of those vivid memories etched in his mind.

He was just nine years old, and his stepfather had gone hunting with his older brother and a friend. They had just gotten home and were out back cleaning two ducks they had killed earlier in the day. Pierce was too young to go with them and had felt really left out. He and his sister had walked into his parents' bedroom where his stepfather had left his shotgun in the corner. He saw it leaning there and could not resist picking it up and holding it in his hand. He sat on the edge of the bed with his little sister beside him and liked the feeling of holding the gun. He lifted the gun up and trembled as the excitement of holding it and the sheer weight combined to make it difficult to hold. The barrel of the gun was just inches from his sister's head. The sheer weight of it caused him to lower it back down so the barrel rested on the bed, and he looked down at the hammer on top of the gun. He used his thumb, and though it was difficult for his small hands to manage, he pulled the hammer back and heard it click in the back position. He smiled at his sister and moved his finger to the trigger and gently pulled it. There was a deafening sound in the bedroom as the shotgun fired and nearly knocked him off the edge of the bed. He stared at his sister in horror as smoke rose from the large hole in the mattress made by the gun. It would be some time before he realized how lucky he was that the smoldering hole was only the mattress and nothing more. In a state of panic, surprise, and that kid logic of immediate denial, he put the gun back in the corner with wisps of smoke still coming from the barrel as well as the hole in the bed. He and his sister ran to the living room, and there was an immediate flurry of activity as the adults rushed in to find out what had happened. His reaction of "what loud noise" and attempts at plausible denial soon gave way to a tear-filled admission of guilt. It helped that his stepfather was genuinely aware of his own fault in leaving the gun loaded and certainly grateful that the only real harm was suffered by a mattress with a gaping wound. It was one of those memories that brought both a smile and a shudder of "what if?"

But as he looked to his left, he was startled once again. During the night, a large spider had built a web from the tree he was now a prisoner of and a smaller tree just to the left of his foot. The spider was less than six inches from his face. He could see the detail of its body, and although he felt the repulsion, his own body was simply too weak to move. He thought about blowing the spider to try to get it to move away, but the tape that was covering his mouth would not allow even that. He would have shuddered from the sight, but he simply had no energy left to move. The spider would be just another reminder of how helpless his situation had become.

The next couple of hours were both painful and frightening as Pierce sat listening to his racing heart and trying to calm himself. His blood was thickening even more from dehydration, and the sound of his heart was increasingly taking over his ability to think about anything else. He tried to force himself to think differently, and he wondered what Sam was thinking. He would have called the cell phone by now and probably called Lynn as well. He hated that they would both be worried about him but felt sure they were looking for him, and it was just a matter of time before they would find him, and all this would be over. But had he told either of them of the route he was taking? How would they know where to look? Had his bike been found yet? Why hadn't that stupid kid called like he said he would?

Just as he was feeling all the frustration building, a butterfly landed on his knee and sat there slowly moving its wings. It had a very calming effect.

He had read not long after losing his sister that if you were visited by a cardinal or a bright butterfly, it was a sign of a lost loved one. He wasn't sure he believed that, but it was a nice thought just the same. And now, this butterfly was comforting for a few moments and had a calming effect as he drifted once again into unconsciousness.

He was out for some time and then struggled back through his increasingly withered state to a point of veiled consciousness. Pierce was struggling to focus. He tried yet again to shift his weight to find relief from the painful torment, but like all of the times before, this attempt brought only a different pain, and he winced and did his level best to relax. How long had he been here?

Pierce saw the reflection of something half-hidden in the dirt. He wasn't sure if it was glass or maybe metal, but even in the shadowy sunlight filtered through the thick leaves of the trees, it reflected a glimmer of sunlight. He wondered if it might be a coin. His mind drifted to that day when he and his son were on their discovery trip out west and had come upon a hiking trail that seemed intriguing. They had been traveling through Big Bend National Park in south-western Texas—miles and miles of a beautifully desolate landscape. They came to a hiking trail called the Lost Mine Trail. It looked very intriguing and a bit of a challenge since it was a five-mile loop that ascended from the beginning at 6100 feet to a vista at 7628 feet. At the beginning of the trail, there was a sign warning of the danger that the area had both mountain lions and bears. It gave instructions to wave your arms frantically and scream loudly if you should encounter either, and they joked that those instructions would not be hard to follow.

Though a bit strenuous, the hike was beautiful, and the views along the trail caused them to pause numerous times. The sky was clear and bright, and they could see for miles as they looked south across the Rio Grande and into Mexico. They walked on until they found themselves at the end of the trail and standing at a magnificent vista that gave them views that seemed almost endless. They sat there on a large rock for quite some time. Neither spoke; they just took in the wonder and staggering splendor of it all—a father and his son on an adventure of a lifetime.

After a short while, they began to talk about the majesty of it, and Pierce felt a little overwhelmed by the reality of his good fortune. An idea occurred to him, and he searched in his pocket to find the few coins that he knew were there. He was elated to find a brand-new nickel that looked so new it might have been minted just yesterday. He smiled at the treasure in his hand that was marked with the current year and held it out to show his son. He began to discuss with him just how fortunate they were to be in that very spot, on that day. His son smiled and showed him once again that though he was only twelve years old, he had an old soul's understanding that made him such a unique young man. They traveled back down the trail a short distance and found two very large rocks that came together in a V, and at the bottom, they moved a rock shaped like a football and placed the shiny coin underneath. Pierce turned to his son and said, "Just maybe, you will bring your twelve-year-old son here one day and find this coin so that you too can realize what a treasure it is to spend such precious time together with your son." And with a hug and a brushed-away tear that Pierce kept to himself, they made their way back down the trail and got back on the road carrying the promise of more adventuring and the prospect that one day the legacy might be continued.

The next time Pierce was awake, he knew the situation was very serious. It was increasingly difficult to breathe, and it felt as if his tongue was filling his whole mouth. The pounding of his heart was still there but did not feel as strong, and already, he had habituated to it.

He started to get angry with himself as he thought about letting that kid get away with this. He could have probably taken him down, and he would not be in this situation. He just had no idea it would come to this. When the kid was winding the tape around his wrists again and again, he didn't have the gun in his hand. Why wasn't he more aggressive, and why didn't he at least try? Was the gun even loaded? And then, he told himself how useless these thoughts were now. The "what-ifs" and "if only" thoughts were never helpful. And it was there, in that quiet stillness that he recognized the true weight and tragedy of every door he had left unopened. Where would he find himself today if he had simply pushed through just one more? And the torture was not the prize he missed, but the guilt of not having simply gone and peered into what was possible. There is no shame in it.

As he tried to get his muddled mind to piece together the time that had passed, Pierce realized that this was the evening of the third day. He recalled a survival show he had watched not long ago that had noted the rule of threes. The average person can go just three minutes without oxygen, three days without water, and three weeks without food. This was his third day, and it was hot and humid. He was indeed aware that his body was shutting down and could not last much longer. He had no strength to attempt to struggle any longer, and the pain was masked by his weakness. He no longer even felt the discomfort of the endless mosquito bites that had been so uncomfortable that first night. Lucid thought was difficult now, and there was an odd peace that came over him as he accepted the likely reality that he was going to die here behind this rock.

But then again, he had to wonder, *why not this day and why not here?* We all share the same inevitable fate, and this was just simply the doorway he had to pass through. This life had been good to him in many ways, and though he never imagined his end would be anything like this, the truth is none of us know. He would have liked to have had one more chance to tell the people he loved just how special they were to him. But for the most part, we all fall short of that goal at one point or another in our lives.

Pierce thought about Lynn. What an incredible gift her presence in his life had been. In his mind's eye, he vividly remembered the last evening he spent with her. He had gone inside the house, and when he returned, she was standing on the deck with the last magical rays of the setting sun behind her. She was wearing a cotton sundress, and the sun pierced the fabric revealing the outline of her figure below. The light gave her hair an iridescent glow. She was absolutely stunning, and for a few seconds, he was stopped in his tracks. When she turned to see him standing there, she smiled. The reality that this sensual beauty was his seemed too good to be true. At that moment, he would have smiled if he could. He could almost feel her soft skin and the fire that came from her lips. The way her eyes sparkled with depth and joy was a moving sight. He could not be more fortunate to have known the greatest and deepest love of his life, and maybe, it was fitting somehow that it would be his waning lucid thoughts. For the last time, in those quiet lonely woods, Pierce lost consciousness, and his body went limp.

Taylor and Emily

TAYLOR AND EMILY were young and had been seeing each other for a few months. They both loved to go hiking in the woods, and they especially liked exploring places they had never been to before. Taylor's dad had told him about a park area that was very seldom used called Forty Acre Rock that was less than an hour away. It had quite a few trails and a very unique rock formation that was not quite forty acres but was an interesting site just the same. On a clear but warm Wednesday morning in July, they set out to do some adventuring.

They traveled down 601 South and eventually came to the brown sign that indicated a park area; it said Forty Acre Rock with an arrow pointing to the right. It was a sharp right turn and then a couple of hundred yards to a gravel parking area on the left. They confirmed what Taylor's dad had said about not being used much since theirs was the only car in the lot.

They found the trail that connected to the parking area and headed out down the trail hand in hand. They had only gone about two hundred yards when Emily looked at Taylor and, while looking down demurely, said, "I need to go." He smiled at her and said, "Well, it doesn't appear there are any facilities here so as I see it, there are two choices: we can get back in the car and find the next store, maybe a restaurant, or you can be a true outdoorsman and go behind one of those big rocks up there." She hesitated only for a second, looked around in all directions, and said, "I will be right back." She headed up the hill toward the two large rocks. Taylor watched as she disappeared between them and, then, being the gentlemen he was raised to be, looked in the direction of the trail. He was glad they had decided to come out today and do some exploring. It would be hot later but was not too bad this morning. A smile came over his face but was quickly erased just a moment later when he heard Emily scream loudly and call out to him. He ran as quickly as he could up the hill to where she stood in shocked disbelief. She stood there frozen looking to her left behind one of the rocks and said, "I think he is dead." He ran up beside her and could not believe his eyes. The sight that had made her scream was a man. He was bound with duct tape and thick bungee cords to a tree and was not moving. He did not appear to be breathing. Taylor called out to him several times and then cautiously moved toward him. He gently raised the man's head and felt his neck for a pulse. He could not feel anything. The man was not breathing, and he could not believe that this poor unfortunate soul was indeed dead. Emily had already pulled her phone from her pocket and was dialing 911. She explained to the operator what they had found and where they were and was told to stay put and that help was on the way. Taylor put his arms around Emily, and she began to cry.

Within minutes, there were first responders running up the trail, and Taylor had moved to the opening between the rocks so he could see when someone came. Taylor was waving frantically for them to come up to where they had found the body. The responders looked at the man and cut the tape from his mouth and hands. They detected no breathing and could not find a pulse. Sadly, there was nothing they could do. He was indeed dead. One of the two stood up and asked what happened, and as Taylor was telling him how they discovered the body, a siren from an ambulance was getting closer. Soon, there was gravel flying as the ambulance arrived with an abrupt stop, and the EMTs rushed down the trail carrying their gearboxes. When they got to the man's side, one of the volunteer firemen who had arrived first on the scene said to the EMT, "He's gone." They opened their cases and began to examine him, and remarkably, one said, "I have a very faint pulse; it isn't much, but it is there." They began working feverishly to cut away the remainder of the constraints and set up an IV with one of them holding the bag up above the man's head. As he held the bag, he barked at the two volunteer responders to go back and get the gurney and hurry! The chance that this guy would make it was very slim, but they would do all they could to see that he had a fighting chance. As they attempted to move him from the tree, they noted his shoulder was grossly out of its socket.

There was no identification of any kind on this John Doe, and he was wearing nothing but a pair of gym shorts.

As they worked to get him on the stretcher that the first responders had retrieved from the ambulance, a county officer appeared around the edge of the rock and began to ask Taylor and Emily questions. He asked the EMTs if the man was alive, and they remarked, "Barely. We need to get him to the hospital right away if he has any chance at all." As the EMTs and first responders struggled to get the man strapped securely to the gurney, one of them was already talking to the hospital to let them know the situation and to be prepared for them when they arrived. The four of them worked together to carry the stretcher down the hill and get it back to the waiting vehicle.

Pierce was brought to KershawHealth Hospital and was quickly evaluated and sent to a room in ICU. He was a man on the brink of death, but the dedicated staff was feverishly working to address his condition. His most immediate need was to turn the tide on his dehydration that had become so serious that his organs, including his heart and his brain, may be damaged. Intravenous fluids had been started by the paramedics, and that would be the most important thing they could do at this point. They had pushed his swollen shoulder back into its socket and bandaged it so he could lie flat on the hospital bed. Now, it was simply a waiting game to see if this extremely weak heartbeat would get stronger and allow the rest of his body to begin to respond as well.

It was late Wednesday afternoon.

The police were already checking to see if there were any missing person reports in the local area, but there were none to fit this man's description. They would get his fingerprints and see if anything came up when they ran them.

For a person who is severely dehydrated, there is a remarkable metamorphosis that occurs as the body absorbs the life-renewing fluids from the IV bags. As the afternoon turned to evening, Pierce was already getting stronger, and though still unconscious, the medical staff were very encouraged by the improvement. By early the next morning, he was fading in and out of consciousness and for brief seconds even opened his eyes.

When the doctor on call came in to check on him, he stood over Pierce and talked to him. He used his flashlight to shine it into his eyes and remarked to the nurse that his pupils were responsive. He listened to his heart and noted it was much stronger. It would take some time to determine if any real damage was done, but it appeared at this point that Pierce was recovering nicely.

As this Thursday wore on, the staff talked about the mystery man brought in yesterday and wondered who he was and where he called home. By lunchtime, they would get their answer.

Pierce came to and drifted softly back into the world. He became aware that he was in the hospital. He heard footsteps in the hall and muted conversation but felt heavy in the bed and not strong enough to move. His eyes were open, and a bright-eyed nurse walked in and said, "Well, hello there. Nice to see you, sir." Pierce struggled to speak to her. He managed a low scratchy, "Hi." She moved his bed to sit him up just a little and asked if he wanted water. He gave a slight nod to indicate he would like a drink. She gently held the cup and the straw up to his lips while telling him to just a little and swallow slowly.

After a couple of sips, he took a moment and then looked at her and asked where he was. She told him the details of which hospital he was in and how he was brought in. By now, there were two other nurses in the room, and the on-call doctor had been notified. As the minutes passed, Pierce was more able to speak in short sentences. He asked if his wife was there, and that is when the nurse told him they did not even know his name and how he came to be tied up in the woods like he had been or how long he had been there. He said, "My name is Pierce Ellis. I was robbed—motorcycle got stolen—and left in the woods by a young kid. The nurses all looked at each other as the pieces started to come together. Over the next couple of hours, Pierce got steadily stronger. When he could speak, his voice was very hoarse, but he said, "I must call my wife; she must be worried sick." Just as one of the nurses was reaching for the phone, two police officers walked into the room.

The officers ran through a series of questions to put together how everything had occurred. It was quite a story by any standard, and they were very sure of one thing: this gentleman was incredibly lucky to be alive. Once they had all they needed, the officers wished Pierce a speedy recovery and said they would be in touch.

It was another day for Lynn of pushing herself to do what needed to be done. She was staring off into space as she sat on the deck when her phone started ringing. She looked down to see a number she did not recognize. For a brief moment, she considered not answering it but reluctantly picked up her phone. The voice on the other end was an officer who identified himself as being assigned to work on her husband's case, and he said, "Ma'am, I have some very unexpected but amazing news regarding your husband Pierce Ellis. He is alive." Lynn found herself trembling as she listened to the officer describe what they understood to be the unbelievable chain of events. She screamed into the phone, "Are you sure?" He confirmed that they were indeed sure and gave her the hospital details. Lynn thanked the officer profusely, and as she did so, she was already going inside to grab her purse and keys and headed out the door.

As soon as she hung up the phone, it began to ring again with another number she did not recognize. Just as she pulled out of the driveway and into the street, her hello was answered by a voice she never thought she would hear again. It was a bit hoarse, but the quiet tears turned into sobs of joy, and she was forced to pull off the road. They talked and cried. They both laughed when she told Pierce about Sam's gesture with the loofah sponge and how it had helped her get through the service. They both became silent for a few moments as the reality of the young man who had been mistakenly buried in Pierce's place caused them to reflect on that morose reality.

She finally gathered herself enough to get back on the road to the hospital, and they talked most of the way there until the doctor came in to check on Pierce.

Two weeks later, Pierce was home. He was sitting on the front porch with Sam, and they were discussing all the crazy stuff that had happened. Pierce had learned the details of the entire story and the tragedy of Jeremy's short life.

As the two old friends sat and talked, Pierce said with a wry smile, "So, when is the next trip?" Sam looked at Pierce and said, "Soon, I hope, but this time I am meeting you here. You don't travel well alone." Pierce looked down a little and groaned, "That, my friend, is probably a very good choice." And with a clink of agreement from their glasses of sweet tea, they turned to watch the sunset.

About the Author

FROM A VERY early age, Loyd Pennington loved a good story. Whether he was listening to them or reading them or sharing one, it was both escape and food for the imagination. His life experiences have included military service and several entrepreneurial pursuits. He is a lifelong student of the wonders of the human experience and enjoys interacting with people from all walks of life. He is always thankful for those who are kind enough to read his words and loves feedback as well. His personal philosophy is that our lives have so few things we "have to do" and so much we "get to do." He speaks often to groups about recognizing and celebrating the difference.